THE CASSANDRA GROUP

MEDDLING WITH FUTURE HISTORY

THE CASSANDRA GROUP
MEDDLING WITH FUTURE HISTORY

JOSEPH A. BONELLI

SUNSTONE
PRESS

SANTA FE

Sunstone books may be purchased for educational, business, or sales promotional use. For information please write: Special Markets Department, Sunstone Press, P.O. Box 2321, Santa Fe, New Mexico 87504-2321.

Book and cover design › R. Ahl
Printed on acid-free paper

Library of Congress Cataloging-in-Publication Data

Names: Bonelli, Joseph A., 1942- author.
Title: The Cassandra group : meddling with future history / by Joseph A. Bonelli.
Description: Santa Fe : Sunstone Press, [2019] | Summary: "In this speculative socio-political novel, a think tank is enlisted to help the president of the United States in sensitive negotiations with a foreign power and their nuclear threat by locating hidden missile sites but with mixed results"-- Provided by publisher.
Identifiers: LCCN 2019032700 | ISBN 9781632932716 (paperback)
Subjects: LCSH: United States--Foreign relations--Korea (North)--Fiction. | Political fiction.
Classification: LCC PS3602.O657156 C37 2019 | DDC 813/.6--dc23
LC record available at https://lccn.loc.gov/2019032700

WWW.SUNSTONEPRESS.COM

SUNSTONE PRESS / POST OFFICE BOX 2321 / SANTA FE, NM 87504-2321 /USA
(505) 988-4418 / ORDERS ONLY (800) 243-5644 / FAX (505) 988-1025

PREFACE

This is a work of fiction. Some of the characters are fictitious, others are well-known, but much despised real people. The interaction between these two sets of people is entirely fictitious and a product solely of the author's turgid imagination. Some of the mountains and Chinese restaurants named herein are real, others imaginary. Some facts and events are historically accurate, others fictional.

Warning: If you have a narrow emotional and intellectual comfort zone, snap this book shut right now. Don't say I didn't warn you. You've already read too far.

This is not fake news. No one put me up to this. If you give me a stack of Bibles as high as I can stand on, I'll swear on them that no Russian troll meddled with my brain, or any other part of me. What's here is speculative history but not "fake." If this offends, and you believe like Candide, that the present state of world affairs is the best that it could be, then I have nothing for you but pity.

Note to the Reference Cataloguers at the Library of Congress: this is a Political Fantasy. This makes your accurate labeling of primary content difficult since there is so little distinction between these two core entities these days. But, everybody's got it tough. Adjust!

< 7 >

The Cassandra Legend

(Updated for Modern Tastes)

Back in the mists of time, there was once a royal princess named Cassandra. Her parents were Priam and Hecaba. They ruled a mighty and rich country called Troy.

The folk there lived on the Gold Standard; no paper money was allowed. A hip and haughty super-hero type named Apollo took an interest in this princess. To win her love he gave her the gift of prophecy. Cassandra thought this was cool but she didn't like the dude so she gave his amatory advances the cold shoulder. Did the dude take back what he had given? No. He just put a curse on her so no one would believe her true prophecies. You got to watch out for these sneaky bad dudes.

"It is only those who have neither fired a shot nor heard the shrieks and groans of the wounded who cry aloud for blood, more vengeance, more desolation. War is hell."
—William Tecumseh Sherman

< 8 >

1

Dark Dawn over Pyongyang

Carlos felt a bit dizzy as he closed the door to his room, yet he didn't forget to shove the heavy mini-carpet under the door to the hallway to keep the rats from entering during the night. This was student intern and low-level government worker housing in Washington, DC. Not much had changed, he thought, since George Washington's time.

He fell onto his bed fully clothed. Then, nothing.

Darkness was in the eyes and hearts of the stunned survivors on the edge of the city. The flashes and the noise were gone. The mushroom-shaped clouds had become formless and were blowing away. The shiny new city center of Pyongyang was bright now with nuclear fires and pockmarked by huge steaming craters. It was a moonscape where pretty, young lady cheerleaders had once danced—and confident soldiers pranced. Carlos had been there only last year.

The dead and dying numbered in the hundreds of thousands, perhaps millions. Hiroshima once more times ten. No memorials would ever be erected here—in this century. In this two thousand-year-old place that was no more. How was this possible? How was he seeing all this? And more importantly why had it happened?

A hell-mix of blood, smoke, and the sounds of human anguish wafted over the charnel fields. U.S. Satellite images picked up only the visuals, of course. No technology existed yet to pick up distant auditory input. Some techies at government installations, viewing this historic moment without soundtrack, showed their humanity by upchucking in sympathy.

Those specially trained to interpret these images knew there was no human pain at ground zero or in the hot-kill zone. Human suffering began at the edges of the blast zone where most people would willingly beg for a bullet to the brain if they could be lucky enough to get one. Where was the NRA when you needed them?

< 9 >

Beyond this zone, there would be survivors. The North Koreans were a tough people both individually and culturally. There would be "Hwarang" survivors (Knights of the Flowers). This Hermit Kingdom had been threatened, bullied, and beaten up by every major power in the area—and by others overseas. There was China, Russia, Japan, and the Western Powers—including U.S. Marines, a long time before that U.N. "Police Action" that started in 1950. Mostly Korea has had no friends, just ex-enemies.

Something in Carlos' brain whispered, "This is not happening. Wake up!"

Tens of thousands lay dead and cremated in Seoul and Tokyo. The pictures looked like a miniature of the destruction at Pyongyang. Surprisingly, each of those cities took hits from only one small nuclear bomb. Apparently, the North Koreans had been partially honest—most of the ICBMs were aimed at the U.S. The crowded nature of these two cities insured the hits would create massive damage as well as incalculable suffering and wailing beyond the edges of the blast zone.

The DMZ and points south were scorched earth and became the instant crematorium of several thousand American soldiers. Guam's airbase was a shambles: three B-1s were expensive scrap and two U.S. aircraft carriers were sunk by missiles. Hawaii basked in the sun... except for Kauai which was wreathed in smoke. Beyond Hawaii there were nine black holes on the North American continent.

Suddenly, Carlos awoke, screaming, "I saw the city burning! Pyongyang is burning! We nuked it!"

"Shaddup in there! Go ta sleep!" came an angry voice through the left wall of his room, punctuated with a hard rap on the wall.

Carlos groggily realized he must have been talking in his sleep. He drank a glass of water, not knowing what else to do, and drifted off again.

He awoke with a hangover. This is impossible, he thought. Two glasses of champagne last night couldn't have given me a hangover. Someone must have spiked the punch at the South Korean Embassy party last night. He used his hotpot to make two cups of coffee and hot oatmeal. Feeling better, he called his Korean friend Choe on his cell. Choe bunked at another residence a few blocks away.

< 10 >

"Choe, what's up?" Carlos asked. "Did you get sick last night by any chance?"

"Sick as a running dog, Carlos. And we're not alone. Someone put LSD in the brownies."

"LSD? That's heavy-handed. They must not have known how to make proper Alice B. Toklas brownies. That's what gave me a bizarre, screaming nightmare last night. I dreamed someone had nuked Pyongyang!"

"Not Seoul?" Choe asked.

"That too! And Tokyo."

"A Dr. Strangelove bad trip."

"Good one, Choe," Carlos said. "Sounds like political sabotage. Does anyone know who did it or why?"

"Not so far, but I'll keep you posted. Good thing you ate only one brownie, Carlos. I ate three of them. Serves me right for my sweet tooth. Once I upchucked I felt better. You ready for Monday?"

"Por cierto, amigo," replied Carlos. "I'll see you at work tomorrow. They don't want me to report until ten a.m. Got laundry to do, food to buy, and need to call home. Like E.T."

"Bravo Carlos," Choe said.

Carlos and Choe were both old friends and old movie fans. They had a running contest to introduce as many references to old movies in their everyday conversation as they could. Such are the strange and myriad manifestations of friendship.

Both Carlos and Choe were moderately handsome with pleasing, outgoing personalities in social situations. Carlos had brown eyes, brown hair, and was exactly six-feet tall. Choe was black-haired with brown eyes, and stood five-feet eleven, which was tall for a South Korean, and a giant compared to North Koreans (who had shrunk due to perennially poor nutrition). Both were near one-hundred eighty pounds, most of the time, depending on their eating habits and exercise opportunities. Yet, despite their social skills, both were essentially introverts; most of their mental energy was spent on reading and thinking about their one true love, history. They could be compared to an iceberg with most of its mass under water. The social skills part was the above-water visible iceberg; the really important part was below the surface.

They had been best buddies for six years. Carlos had spent a

< 11 >

whole summer with the Yi family in Seoul and Choe had spent a whole summer with Carlos' family in rural New Mexico near Santa Fe and close to the Pojoaque Pueblo. They had fought with each other for years. Both men were fifth Dan Tae Kwon Do black belts. They were both world historians and experts on Korean history and came from famous families.

Choe was a descendant of Korea's most famous naval hero, Admiral Yi Sansin. Sansin invented the world's first iron-clad warships to protect against the then deadly attack by fire arrows. Carlos' family settled in northern New Mexico at the same time (1598) Admiral Yi was fighting off the Japanese invasion fleet and sending Hideyoshi home.

One of Carlos' granddaddies had been an officer at the tiny Arizona fort of Santa Cruz de Terrenate in the famous summer of 1776, barely beating off a vigorous multi-day attack by local Apaches who had little fear of Spanish cannons and muskets.

Carlos' full name was Carlos Ordoñez Longoria but he had changed it simply to "Numantia." Numantia is a famous place in Spain where the Celto-Iberians withstood a Roman siege for twenty-five years, before being annihilated and having their city sown with salt.

Carlos was no recent immigrant to these shores; his people beat the Pilgrims here. He was touchy about being called a Hispanic because that term had been politicized by too many gasbags.

Choe's full name was Choe Yi Sansin but he usually was just known as plain Choe Yi. Choe was a modest fellow and felt that walking about with the "Sansin" moniker was too much like bragging. Not that anyone would have bothered him; he looked like a tall version of Bruce Lee's brother.

< 12 >

2

CARLOS THE WOLF MEETS THE GENERAL

March 26, 2018
The Pentagon, Day 1

It was a historian's dream—to be allowed to observe and participate personally in the making of history—and starting today, Carlos Numantia was living that dream. This was his first day of employment at the Pentagon as a strategic historian, assigned to the six-person "Cassandra Group" which advised policymakers of likely effects of various military actions, or inactions.

An exciting time, Carlos thought, because history was in the making as preparations got underway for serious negotiations involving both Koreas and the U.S., and a face-to-face meeting between the leaders of the U.S. and North Korea. Only a couple days ago, Mr. Pompeo had been selected as the Secretary of State to give the president a stronger team. Carlos' political leanings were as neutral as any person's could be in this tumultuous time (to protect his professional objectivity and his sanity). He was now a member of the president's team.

In the first week Carlos arrived, the Cassandra Group met regularly. They were given a simplistic but futile exercise. They were to line out a possible land war option with North Korea, eschewing the use of air and navy actions—and no utilization of nukes. The group, including Carlos the newcomer, rebelled at this sophomoric exercise. The group leader was a bland, and not too bright, stuffed shirt, political appointee.

This was not the first dumb dork Carlos had ever worked for, but it hurt every time. He was starting to have second thoughts about this job by the end of the first day. However, he decided to give it a chance and suspend judgment for a while.

By Wednesday, he noticed that the group's military historian, General Otis Callahan, was friendly to him and Choe and the other

< 13 >

historian, Charles Mandrake, but did not care for the economist or diplomat members of the team.

Callahan never answered to "Otis" and few people were gauche enough to try calling him by his first name. And "Otis" didn't give you a lot to work with if you wanted a nickname unless you were a horse. Callahan was thin and stood erect at six-feet two inches. He wore a typical, short military haircut and the confident bearing of a military man or athlete (he was both). Carlos thought he looked about fifty but an early remark he had made historically tagged him at age sixty-one or above. His pleasant gray eyes saw most everything going on around him and his sharp ears (though not as good as Carlos') heard most everything. He reminded Carlos of Alan Quatermain. He often chatted with Carlos in Spanish. He had served in a Spanish-speaking war zone where he acquired a serviceable knowledge of the language.

At the end of a boring meeting on the last day of the first week, General Callahan took Carlos aside after the meeting broke up and walked with him towards the employees' lounge.

"Dr. Numantia, do you have a few minutes? I would like to fill you in on some background on this Cassandra Group."

"Certainly General, where do you suggest we have this conversation?"

General Callahan pointed to some vacant chairs nearby. "Let's just sit here. We won't bother anyone and won't look like we're planning a coup. Even though I am."

"Madre Mia, General. This is exciting," Dr. Numantia said with a smile.

"Carlos, this group was conceived by a bipartisan coalition during the Obama Administration. That's why it's still functioning. However, I know the president doesn't like it because it isn't giving him something he can use, especially with the Korea meetings coming up this May with Kim and company. It's just another unfocused committee. I'm going to stick my neck out and ask him to drop me from the group, appoint me in place of that cardboard political appointee, drop the economist and diplomat and focus us historians into being "predictive historians" that can give him strategic predictions of military outcomes resulting from possible sanctions we might use—or threats of sanctions."

"General, your ambition amazes me and refreshes me. I like your ideas. I'm your man. This makes me want to stay here. Viva Zapata!"

Carlos didn't know it yet, but his second week of work would not

< 14 >

start with a whimper, but a bang. Was this flipping around business the work of God—or the Malcolm Effect? Man craves predictability and control. What was out there waiting? Coyote? Chaos? Godot? The Wheel of Fortune? Same thing, just different labels.

< 15 >

3

Carlos and the Angel

April 2, 2018
Walter Reed Hospital/10:00 a.m.

Carlos awoke slowly, groggy and confused. A young lady with a white cap and a grim smile said she was a nurse and that he was in Walter Reed Hospital. He finally knew where he was. The little voice in his head said, "Stay cool, Carlos, you'll figure it all out." And he did. He remembered how he had gotten here. He was not pleased to see a whole bunch of strangers hovering around his bed. He hated hospitals. He was not happy with the thought that he had been blown up on the first day of his second week at his new job. How inconsiderate of the Fates.

Dr. Cleveland, a burly black man in his mid-fifties asked, "How are you feeling?"

"Glad to be awake, doctor. Got a bad headache and I feel like shit, but I think I'll live. Who are all these people? They're not anybody I know."

"Do you know what your name is and how you got here?" Dr. Cleveland asked.

"Sure. I'm Carlos Numantia. I'm a historian from Stanford and I was blown up at the Pentagon while reporting for my sixth day of work for the Cassandra Group. On the morning of Monday April second. I hope this is still Monday."

Dr. Cleveland turned to the waiting group, "Gentlemen and lady, you may go ahead and talk to him. Just don't tire him. And yes, it's still Monday the second."

Instinctively, Carlos knew he was talking to two Secret Service agents and a shrink. They identified themselves as Agent Barkley, Agent Hidalgo, and Dr. Sally Sarandon.

At first, the agents were vaguely suspicious of him but after a

< 16 >

while that subsided as he talked to them cogently and extensively. Carlos suspected that some bigwig was in the group he had been approaching when the action began. He was now being told that it was the president himself; he had narrowly missed assassination by three antifa radicals using wheelchair bombs.

So those left-wing Nazi thugs who beat up everyone with an opinion opposite theirs were responsible for the worst headache I've ever had, thought Carlos. All these creeps preaching diversity—except in political thought.

He remembered noticing in his peripheral vision, as he had walked toward the president's group, two wheelchairs being wheeled a little too fast down converging paths. There was a strange whistling in his head and he hunkered behind a statue while his conscious mind tried to make sense of things. One of the agents close to the president had taken this cue to push the president down. Both the president and Agent Barkley had heard the deadlier whistle of shrapnel over their heads. Now Carlos and Agent Barkley were heroes for the day. The president didn't even change his regular schedule, just went on with what he had been doing, as a new cadre of agents whisked him away from the grounds. No media was present so rumors of what had happened only reached Fox News hours later. CNN thought it all fake news and the media giants ignored it as well.

Dr. Sarandon talked to him more a little later in the morning, having first visited a veterinarian friend of hers and borrowing a dog whistle with which she tested Carlos' hearing. Her report which had been specifically ordered by someone in the White House summarized: "Subject is highly intelligent, clearly in the genius category. He has strong survival instincts, able to quickly assess risks around him. His hearing is beyond human norms; he can hear sounds made by dog whistles. Dog whistles, or some similar device, were used in the attack. He may be both highly intuitive and a bit paranoid. He has a nearly eidetic memory and if science ever discovers there is anything to this Sixth Sense business, I would say that Dr. Numantia has it."

Dr. Sarandon faxed the report to the White House immediately upon its completion.

At three-thirty that Monday afternoon, the president visited Carlos at the hospital, along with Agent Barkley, and thanked him for helping save both their lives. After the president left, Nurse "Grim" came in and told him that Dr. Cleveland didn't want him returning to

< 17 >

work until Thursday but he was free to go home.

At four o'clock as Carlos was being released from the hospital, in walked Dr. Sarandon. She looked very good indeed. She was five-feet six inches, blonde, looked great in a white doctor's coat, and had a sunny disposition and warm smile. Carlos was certain she was a "reader," not someone who read those cockamamy books on the Bestsellers List or Oprah's, but someone who could quickly read people's thoughts from their body language and what they say about themselves unguardedly and even openly. Carlos had no dark secrets—he didn't mind being read by someone as attractive as she. Little did he know, opportunity was knocking.

"Can I give you a lift someplace, Dr. Numantia?"

"Oh, no thanks. I can get home on my own, I think."

"Please, let me take you out of here. This is a pickup. I'm making a pass at you. You're really not my regular patient and I want to know you…socially."

Ten seconds of stunned silence ticked away. And then Carlos said with a smile, "Let's go."

"You like Chinese food?" she asked. "I know a hole in the wall called The Red Dragon, a place tourists haven't found yet. It's sort of near L'Enfant Plaza but it doesn't want to be found. A Chinese patient of mine told me how to find it."

"Great!" said Carlos, all the while thinking it sounded like the Zodiac Club in *Bell, Book, and Candle*. Maybe Sally was a witch too. It had only taken her two minutes to bewitch him.

As they finished dinner, Carlos said, "Sally, this little hole in the wall has got really good food. What a find. Reminds me of a similar place 'The Wokking Panda' in Gardiner, Montana at the northeast end of Yellowstone. Their Mongolian beef is the best you can eat anywhere. Partly because he uses lots of superb Montana beef. The Imperial Gourmet in Bishop is good too and convenient if you're climbing Mount Whitney. And there's a nice Red Dragon in Auburn if you're coming back from skiing at Tahoe. The Mandarin Garden in Page is good if you're doing Lake Powell. But that cook in Gardiner is the best. Too bad he stopped making his Hot and Sour Soup. Probably because some tourist's throat caught on fire. Boy, was that good stuff. That restaurant must be written up in Chinese travel books because some nights Chinese is all you hear."

"You're so sweet, Carlos. I'm going to enjoy getting to know you.

< 18 >

Please stay with me the whole time you have left here. I'm not trying to trap you or anything. I won't get pregnant. I think women who do that are the lowest of the low."

"Just promise to get me to my rooming house door by seven a.m. on Thursday morning and I will try my best to please you. You're the only sane—and nice—shrink I've ever met. And 'Don Juan' is not a role I'm familiar with despite my Spanish heritage."

By Tuesday morning they were both pleasantly exhausted. Marathoners need their rest so they slept in after first seeing the sunrise. They were voraciously hungry and took a little time out to talk after coffee, eggs and every interesting thing in Sally's fridge.

"So, Carlos dear, did you ever think about going into medicine or psychiatry before you decided on history?"

"Sally, here's a secret. My mother was a doctor. She's retired now, but for a short time I had to help her run her office when her receptionist was sick. I was ten. My father was out of the country on a dangerous diplomatic mission. I got to reading simple case histories and I found it fascinating. Of course, my mother wasn't happy about it and explained why I shouldn't do that. I considered psychology and psychiatry when I first started college and even took some advanced courses. Maybe they even helped me get the job that I have now. Maybe they thought my background would make it possible to psychoanalyze Kim Jung On. Administrators are always looking for simple solutions to complex problems. They don't know that it's probably easier to predict the future actions of a country or culture rather than the action of one single complex human being, especially an individual like Kim who comes from a culture of 'Juche' with finishing touches of schooling in Switzerland of all places. Kim is an anomaly in his own country; a young leader in a country that honors the elderly."

"So, Carlos, is there any place you want to go tomorrow?"

"Sweet Sally, I don't care whether we stay here or go somewhere, I just want to be with you. You're the first woman I've ever loved. I'm no back door man."

"I haven't had much experience with this sort of thing either, Carlos. I'm trying to play it right. I'm afraid what little experience I've had is with an egotistical genius—not a decent man like you. I divorced him."

"Good for you," Carlos said.

The rest of the time until seven a.m. on Thursday was mostly

< 19 >

spent feeling and loving—and not talking. If this doesn't sound salacious enough read that book about all the shades of gray. There's a time for everything under the sun. The Bible says that.

< 20 >

4

The Gossipers

Thursday April 5, 2018
The Pentagon/9:00 a.m.

Face it ladies, you have a bad press. Men are just as ambitious gossips as you ladies but you got stuck with the bad rep. I don't know how it happened but you must know life isn't fair. Within an hour Carlos, Choe and Charlie had passed on a slightly discreet chronicle of their separate weekend doings, with Carlos topping everyone this time—even though Choe had a hot date Saturday night with Sultry Sara, the office's computer operator 'man-killer'/coup counter (the opposite of the #MeToo Girl).

Charlie had the low card this time. His major achievement had been to read Hugh Thomas's 1961 classic *The Spanish Civil War*. At any other water cooler that would have merited no more than a yawn, but Carlos was impressed.

"You read that sucker in one weekend? That's real determination, Charlie. That was one of the most confusing wars ever fought—so many factions. The leaders must have needed scorecards."

Sally had told Carlos Wednesday evening that she had a batch of tickets to the zoo that could be used the coming weekend if he wanted to bring his friends and if so she could call some of her lady friends. She even included General Callahan in the invitation as she also had some sharp older lady pals. Afterwards they could go to the Red Dragon.

That weekend excursion turned out well. General Callahan even came. He and a nurse named Mary Lou Shannon hit it off instantly. A tradition was born. Every Saturday night at seven-thirty p.m. you could find the Cassandra Group having dinner at the Red Dragon— assuming you could find the Red Dragon.

< 21 >

April 30, 2018
The New Cassandra Group Emerges

Generally, bureaucracies crank glacially slowly, thought Carlos, as he waited for his meeting to start, but in this case, things were moving at hyper-speed. Callahan's reorganization plan had been approved in a few weeks. So much was happening. John Bolton had been appointed the president's National Security Advisor, and with Mike Pompeo as the Secretary of State, the president was feeling he had a winning team. All three of them were actually coming here today to listen to what the Cassandra Group had to say on North Korea sanctions—in the event the North Koreans would refuse to denuclearize, whatever that meant.

Carlos and his two associates in the Cassandra Group had been waiting over half an hour in the special meeting room set aside for their most distinguished guests. It was good, he thought, to have a little breather because mostly the daily grind was hectic. Read this. Read that. Comment on some memo or document. Write instant memos. Attend meetings. Historians in their normal habitat were a different, quieter animal. Mostly they read books or documents in quiet places, if they could find them.

Today, however, would put them in the big leagues. Carlos looked over at Choe, his friend and their historian from South Korea by way of Harvard, and was rewarded by a rare, shy grin.

"Big Day at Black Rock," Choe said to Carlos. Their historian from Oxford, Charles Mandrake, laughed and said, "Speaking in code, are we?"

"No," Choe replied, "we are speaking in tongues, Charlie."

Charlie blushed, never sure of when he was being made fun of or when someone was "pulling his leg" as the Americans say.

Carlos laughed. "Charlie, Choe and I are both old Hollywood movie fans and have a shared 'Black Rock' experience. So, in a way we're talking in code. And sometimes we have a weird sense of humor, so don't be offended. You might even call us 'Windtalkers.'"

Charles Mandrake was six-foot one, one-hundred eighty-five pounds, a blonde, blue-eyed Briton. He was an all-round athlete, with a smile and laugh that charmed ladies of all ages. Like Carlos and Choe his muse was the love of history; like the other men he was an expert in Korean history though he was a poor linguist and could speak only rudimentary Korean.

< 22 >

Carlos and his mates with regular visits from "El Jefe" (General Callahan) had spent days haggling over the issue of 'military' sanctions and what their effect would be on North Korea when applied. Everyone knew that economic and political sanctions had limited success. As General Callahan entered the room, Carlos asked what was being discussed at higher levels.

"The bigwigs," said Callahan, "are putting political pressure on the president to make some accommodation with Kim because he is no longer acting defiant but meowing like a compliant pussycat. We all know as historians this is the same sophisticated con they have used in the past to get their way. They are repeating Obama's mistakes, as well as Bush's and Clinton's. And so on, backward in time—and thinking."

Choe piped up, "Our Kim is a regular 'Elmer Gantry.'"

Carlos smiled at this quip and said, "Maybe it's our job to convince the president's inner group of that."

"Bolton," said Charlie, "seems to already be convinced of it."

"You're right, Charlie," said General Callahan.

"I wonder why Bolton thinks Iran is so dangerous," Carlos said. "On North Korea I agree with him, but what could Iran do to us? Sure, some of their mid-range missiles could damage our military installations in Turkey and Germany, but they are not real motivated to hurt us. I think they prefer to keep their missiles for Israel and Saudi Arabia. Of course, they could spare us some curses from their ayatollahs but those would do us no more harm than that done by the meddlesome Russian trolls, or the Madison Avenue mavens who feed us ten lies per minute, twenty-four seven."

For several minutes there were smiles followed by several minutes of silence.

Charlie piped up, "General, what's your opinion of this new budget bill the president signed? Some of his supporters say he gave away the store, as you Americans say."

"I don't know, Charles," replied Callahan. "Could be that the president fluctuates back and forth between being a moderate and being a conservative and maybe also a maverick. Of course, liberal Democrats think he's a demon from Hell, or Lucifer himself."

"Or maybe," Choe interjected, "he wants to protect his flank when he deals with Kim Jung On."

< 23 >

Carlos clapped and said, "I vote with Choe on this, but you know it's possible you are both right."

"How about Kim's visit to President Xi Jinping of China?" Charlie said. "That was truly a bold move."

Carlos eyeballed Charlie, "Choe and I have hashed this over thoroughly in view of past Chinese-Korean relations. Korea is 'little brother' to China's 'elder brother' in an unusual political-social relationship that has endured over hundreds of years. Visiting Beijing was an important symbolic and canny political move which was understood by all of Asia."

"This is heap big medicine like they say in those old Cowboy/ Indian movies," Choe said.

< 24 >

5

ENTER NUMERO UNO

The door opened slowly, without a warning knock. Standing in the doorway was an older man and complete stranger who inquired, "Is this the meeting room of the Cassandra Group?"

Luckily, Carlos' nearly eidetic memory instantly gave him a name.

"I believe I am speaking to Defense Secretary Jim Mattis," Carlos said, "and over there is our chief, General Callahan."

Callahan moved quickly to shake Mattis's hand. "I'm sorry I didn't greet you ahead of time, sir. I was not advised you were coming." As he said these words, Callahan was thinking, My God, it's Mad Dog Mattis himself!

Nobody in that room had expected to see Numero Uno come visit them. Callahan had never set eyes on him before this.

"Well," Mattis said, "the president mentioned this meeting to me yesterday, so I thought maybe he wanted me to drop by today."

"Come join us at the table, sir," Callahan said. "We are waiting for the president to arrive—he's been delayed."

"I see. Well that's not unusual. Do you have a written agenda for this meeting?"

"No sir, we don't."

"Will the Iran Agreement be coming up for discussion?"

"Highly unlikely sir. My group's focus is entirely on the North Korea business. For now."

"Is it possible we could find ourselves in a shooting war with North Korea in the near future?"

"Of course, sir. A shooting war is a distinct possibility but not right now. After the negotiations, if they don't get what they want, or if the president gives them too hard a time, then they might think about military moves."

"Well, that's somewhat comforting for now." Mattis replied. "And who are these gentlemen?"

< 25 >

"They are some of the smartest and most knowledgeable up and coming historians in the world. I am just an old war horse with an ancient master's degree in military history with a bit of real-world experience here and there.

"If you ever want my crew to look at the Iran situation for you, we would be happy to do so. We were just talking about how Bolton has a burr under his saddle over Iran and we were trying to figure what danger he sees from them. However, we all think he's dead right about North Korea being an imminent threat to us."

"What about a first strike against North Korea?" Mattis asked. "Do you think he's right about that?"

"I think it's a rational option both strategically and ethically, that needs serious study and should not be discarded out of hand," Callahan replied.

"North Korea has told us all their nukes are aimed at us," Callahan continued. "And we know now that in fact they could reach any place in the continental United States. There is reason to believe that some are right now aimed at Washington, DC, New York and Los Angeles, and other major population centers. Therefore, North Korea is a threat to the security of the U.S. (as John Bolton asserted) and we are therefore justified in using a first strike option without a declaration of war, against all known North Korean Nuclear/ICBM sites. The only downside of this plan is its current political unpopularity."

Mr. Mattis looked thoughtful. "Well," he said, "this is all a lot to think about. Maybe you'll hear from me some day, General."

Mattis rose from his chair suddenly and walked towards the door. "Gentlemen, please tell the president that I came by to say hello and I wish you all well in your endeavor."

Callahan shook Mattis's hand before he exited the room. "It was a pleasure to meet you, sir."

"Likewise, I'm sure," Mattis replied.

For two minutes there was complete silence in the room.

Suddenly, Carlos faced the closed door and said, "Here they come."

Charles Mandrake looked at him dubiously. "How do you know?"

Carlos smiled, "Maybe I'm psychic, Charlie."

Dr. Charles Mandrake replied, "Stop meddling with my mind, Carlos."

< 26 >

Choe smiled at Charlie and said, "Carlos has the nickname 'Wolf' for several reasons, the first is he can hear way beyond human range and nearly into wolf range."

< 27 >

6

ENTER AN ELEMENTAL...AND A PRESIDENT

The door opened and a Secret Service agent poked his head in the door and asked, "Cassandra Group?"

"That's us," replied Choe.

A small entourage entered immediately with the President. Aside from the usual cadre of Secret Service agents there was a stunningly attractive young woman introduced as Delilah Cummings, Special Assistant to Mr. Pompeo. She was a statuesque five-foot nine-inch brunette Amazon. An elemental, Carlos said to himself. All the eyes in the room were riveted on her, for a bit longer than was decorous.

Choe wondered if this was the president's new girlfriend. If so, she made Stormy Daniels look like a has-been matron. Choe loved insider gossip, whether it was movie star memoirs or current day political or society gossip. On second consideration, he thought maybe he's Pompeo's or Bolton's girlfriend. Melania would not tolerate any extramarital hanky-panky like a certain White House wife had in Washington in recent years.

As General Callahan was introducing his staff, the president rose from his chair, walked towards Carlos and shook hands with him. "I know this fella, he and Agent Barkley saved my life about a month ago. How are you these days, Carlos?"

"Just fine, sir. Thank you for your concern."

"Agent Barkley picked up some scuttlebutt that you had a nickname, 'Carlos the Wolf,'" the president said. "Is that because you are such a ladies' man?"

"Oh no, sir," General Callahan answered for Carlos. "He's an old-fashioned gentleman but jokesters tried to give him the name 'Carlos the Jackal' after the famed assassin. Carlos insisted on 'Wolf' because jackals followed whoever fed them but wolves were independent. Nicknames are good for morale, unless they get nasty."

"What's my nickname with your staff, General?" the president asked.

< 28 >

"Hard pants, sir."

The president laughed. "I can wear that!"

After the rest of the formalities and introductions, the president led off the discussion. "So, General Callahan, how tough are the North Koreans? Could we engage them with non-nuclear traditional warfare?"

"Mr. President, we could certainly do so, but the cost would be high. A ballpark figure has been bandied around for years and it would cost us half a million American soldiers."

At this point, Carlos addressed General Callahan, "But sir, this scenario could never be played out now since the North Koreans, as the weaker party, would escalate immediately to their nuclear and ICBM weaponry now that they have it. And they have lots of miscellaneous stuff."

"Is he right, General?" asked John Bolton.

"Yes, sir," Callahan replied.

Choe and Charlie were nodding their heads in agreement with Carlos.

"What exactly do the North Koreans have?" Mr. Pompeo asked.

Carlos responded, "Twenty to sixty nuclear bombs, two hundred short, medium, and long-range launchers, and twenty-five hundred to five thousand tons of chemical weapons."

"Chemical weapons?" asked the president.

"Chemical and biological," replied Choe.

There was a short silence in the room.

"How about a first strike option?" asked Bolton.

"Theirs or ours?" Carlos said.

"Are you saying the North Koreans have a 'First Strike Plan?'"

"Not a written plan in a secret folder. I doubt they are quite like us in that respect, but given the right circumstances, they might and likely would strike us first."

"What circumstances?"

"I can't say for sure. When does a cornered rat turn on its pursuer? If the North Koreans got even a hint we would launch on them tomorrow morning, they would launch on us tonight. Thus, would begin the Second Korean War, and perhaps more."

All the historians at the table nodded in agreement.

Bolton's intensity increased. It was as if he was pissed that the North Koreans might have been the first to think up a first strike

< 29 >

option. "Dr. Numantia, would you and your Cassandra Group know when they reached that point of pressing the first strike button?"

"I am fairly sure we would, sir, as long as we were kept in the loop of ongoing political doings and such. But, for that to work, General Callahan would need higher security clearance than he has now, at least in that subject area. You understand of course we might be talking about a couple of years because those guys are political masters of the stall. They'll do anything they can think of to slow things down. When we do know, it will be past the eleventh hour so there will be little time to act."

"John," said the president, "why don't we do it this way, if the Cassandra Group unanimously think the button is ready to be pushed, they should get a message to me."

"Afghanistan Bananastand," Carlos said.

"What?" the president and Bolton said simultaneously.

"It's an easy to remember code word from a mystery," replied Carlos. "One of my father's favorite authors."

So, it was agreed. (Mr. Westlake would not have minded.)

"Our major concern is discovering where North Korea's hidden nuclear/ICBM launch sites are located," General Callahan said. "They are bound to have at least one or more of them off our radar. They have shielded at least one or more from satellite surveillance from the beginning. Hopefully someone is already working seriously on this problem."

"I don't know of anyone who is, but how do you know these bases exist?" Mr. Pompeo asked. "The CIA and even some of the diplomatic types are warning us of the same thing, but nobody has specific locations or concrete proof, or ideas to find them. Moles are impossible to place. Some of their defectors we have welcomed with open arms in South Korea might be North Korean double agents.

"All we have is deductive reasoning from the historic record plus some vague statements or rumors from low-level defectors. Choe knows lots of the South Korea military folk and they get occasional claims from defectors who say they worked in secret installations. Generally, only the high-level defectors get much attention like Clive."

"Certainly, the CIA already has a list of known North Korean launch bases. If they could share that with us we could tell them if we hear rumors of other locations."

"Mr. President," Mike Pompeo said, "I have a concern here. We

< 30 >

should have wording in any agreement with these people that says if they fail to disclose a hidden launch base the whole agreement is invalidated."

"Mike, that sounds like a winner. They would know we were looking and that we are serious. We don't want to be anybody's patsy on this one."

"I'll make a note to our negotiating group, Mr. President."

"General, could your group handle that chore? Finding the hidden bases?" asked John Bolton.

"The logistics of that would be beyond us, but we could provide some sort of input to help focus the search if someone else had primary responsibility. As an example, Choe suggested if we drop leaflets printed in Korean over known and suspected nuke/ICBM bases we might get a higher defection rate. We could offer gold coins to defecting personnel who know their base is not on the official 'declared' base list. You know the North Koreans are going to hide anything they can. A little capitalism to corrupt the hungry workers might get us what we need to know."

"Good idea," said the president.

"What kind of team do you think is needed to pull off this assignment?" Pompeo asked.

"A geographer/cartographer, maybe even a consulting geologist," Carlos replied.

"A missile site nuclear technician or engineer," Charlie added.

"A CIA experienced operative or intelligence gathering specialist," Callahan said.

"A puzzle person or planner/manager; someone who can figure things out and make them happen," Choe said.

Mike Pompeo made eye contact with Delilah, his Special Assistant. She nodded vigorously in reply.

"Mr. President," Mike said, "my special assistant Delilah Cummings can sit down in one afternoon and put together a five hundred-piece jigsaw puzzle and she has the same organizing abilities as her father."

"See to it, Mike," the president replied. "This project needs high priority. Give it to them and let them run with it. If they find any hidden sites, that intel should be passed on to the Russians and the Chinese so they will know what kind of a sneaky ally they have."

A knock on the door brought the Sandwich Man bearing a tray

< 31 >

of goodies. For five minutes nothing was said and only the sounds of eating could be heard. No one said 'Grace' since there was no lady in the room by that name.

The president signaled for General Callahan to continue.

< 32 >

7

DENUCLEARIZATION AND THE DEVIL'S OWN SANCTION

"Mr. President, before this meeting you asked us to define denuclearization and to list possible sanctions against North Korea if they failed to denuclearize. We have succeeded better with the second half of the assignment. Sanction A is an unannounced first strike against all known North Korean nuclear/ICBM sites. This is Mr. Bolton's plan and we believe it is ethically defendable but politically unpopular, mainly because our own people have not comprehended what a dangerous position we're now in. It would likely be unpopular with China and Russia too."

Callahan continued speaking. "Before we implement Sanction B we must be willing to demand the instant, within three days, simultaneous surrender of all North Korean nuke/ICBM sites to us, with no declaration of war. We launch on their refusal or failure to act. We will launch if they attack first.

"Sanction C we ask Congress for a declaration of war to implement Sanction B. Both B and C would be disliked by Russia and China, setting up a possible start to World War III.

"Sanction D is a draconian sanction we would use only if the U.S. had been attacked first by North Korea and significant damage has been inflicted or is expected to be inflicted on either military or civilian areas. It targets all nuke/ICBM bases throughout North Korea, the city of Pyongyang in its entirety, and all significant military bases throughout North Korea, including repositories of biologicals and chemical weapons. If the North Korea army subsequently heads south toward the DMZ we will nuke that as well.

"Under this sanction, the destruction of Pyongyang, the epicenter of North Korea's fascism, is necessary for total cultural change which goes way beyond simple regime change. Under this sanction we are not looking to displace Kim for a Kim-clone or for a Kim Yong Chul. Nor is this to practice genocide on the North Korean people. We will attempt to root out an insane, diseased, military abomination and

< 33 >

political cancer which has both threatened us as well as the rest of the world and crushed its own people with systematic hunger.

"This is not a fight for democracy, but for humanity. North Korean fascism needs to be destroyed either by the sword or by being corrupted by capitalism and prosperity. That choice will be theirs before this Armageddon sanction is used. Some political figures such as Ron Paul and Rand Paul consider regime change an improper policy for a democratic U.S. We agree with them generally. North Korea is the only exception.

"Of course, if both Russia and China came to believe that they were both targeted by North Korean nuclear missiles, the same as we are, it might be possible to proceed with all sanctions.

"We believe this is actually the case because of North Korea's paranoia toward all, friend and foe alike, but we have no shred of objective proof and such information would be the most carefully guarded secret."

"General Callahan, your Sanction D sounds like the devil's own, but I cannot fault it. Are other sanctions possible?" Bolton asked.

"Other sanctions or negotiations are possible but require more thought and a better understanding of what each side really wants and is willing to bargain over."

"Mr. President," Carlos said, "a word of caution about negotiating with Kim. I'm not sure it's possible at all. I am convinced Kim is a pathological liar as well as a psychopath; the two often go together. A pathological liar unlike most liars is someone who doesn't know they are lying. I've discussed this with my girlfriend who is a practicing psychiatrist and she agrees."

"And," Mr. Pompeo said, "as I understand it Carlos you have some psychiatric background yourself."

"Another complication to consider," added the president. "Well, we'll still have to initially treat him as if he were a rational person."

"Carlos, can you continue the discussion of denuclearization," Callahan asked.

"Yes, sir. This word denuclearization could become a semantic trap for us, a word trap that prevents our expressing what we really want. As we see the problem in its simplest terms, North Korea is holding a gun to Uncle Sam's head and demanding stuff from us and our allies like recognition, economic development, and money. This used to be called piracy or highway robbery. Are these guys that much

< 34 >

different from Somali pirates? What we must do first is grab their gun finger or stick our finger in their gun barrel. Then we empty the bullets in their gun or take it away from them. This is Phase One as we see it. Phase Two is denuclearization, getting rid of the nukes and ICBMs. This might take years to accomplish and presupposes a high level of compliance which they have never shown before.

"The CVID acronym we use these days may have some uses for educating media and diplomats but remember the first three letters are adjectives describing how thorough a denuclearization we want to see at some dim future time, but it can also cloud the more important issue of taking North Korea's fingers off their nuke/ICBM triggers fast and soon. Or we live under perennial blackmail, threats and fear.

"Again, the rest we see as Phase Two, an area more fitting for broader negotiation with a willing party."

"Solely from a military point of view, Mr. Bolton's suggestion of Sanction A is by far the most preferable," Charlie interjected. "It is the one most certain to succeed. The quickest solution. However, American citizens have not yet grasped, with their emotions and brains, that because North Korea is aiming Kwasong-fifteen missiles with a range of fourteen thousand km at U.S. cities, that it is the same level of danger as a freaky kid with a thirty-eight aiming at their children in their local school.

"For too many years the politicians told them there was little to fear from North Korea. Using this option now would result in major political flak from our allies and the United Nations. The bleeding hearts would shed tears all over the place and the Democrats would seriously try to impeach you. And, if there are hidden nuke sites, and they retaliate and hit American cities there will be more hell to pay even though it was all your predecessors' failure to hold the North Koreans to task and their failure to look for and find those hidden sites that put us in this mortal danger."

Carlos spoke next. "When the North Koreans fail to get an economic handout from any quarter, what is to prevent them from playing the 'Pirate Extortion Game' and hitting up Japan for a one-billion-dollar ransom or Tokyo gets nuked, or South Korea for the same or Seoul gets nuked? Or one-third of the rice crop of Thailand, Myanmar and Vietnam, or select cities, get a nuclear facelift? Must horrors of this nature happen before we are willing to force North Korea to instantly divest itself of all their nuclear and missile weaponry?"

< 35 >

"General Callahan, for our next meeting can your group work up for us an E sanction—or something you think we can use," Bolton asked.

"We'll do our best, sir," Callahan replied.

"John, I want to know more about these people we will be sitting down with at the table," said the president, turning to Carlos. "So, Carlos, what are these North Koreans like?"

"Sir, I am understanding you want some sort of psychological profile. The best capsule description of the North Korean psyche was given to me just this morning over the phone by one of your old Korean generals. He said, 'These guys are serious folk, kind of stiff, got no sense of humor, and are paranoid as hell, but perhaps for good historical reason. Everybody in the neighborhood is bigger than them and has beat them up. Prickly as porky-pines if you don't let them save face. Got a touch of the Jap Kamikaze in them too; dangerous as a wounded warthog or cornered rat. They are blackmailers, hustlers, bluffers, and world class liars. They'll come up with any malarkey they think you want to hear to get their way—and won't deliver on any of their promises unless you hold their feet to the fire.'"

Everyone seemed amazed at Carlos' recitation of this monologue.

"Mr. President, you have to understand Carlos has a nearly photographic memory which is very useful for a historian to have," Callahan said.

"General, is there anything else for now?" Pompeo asked.

"Mr. President, we understand that joint U.S./South Korea military exercises have been postponed but will still occur during the period of the talks," Callahan said.

"Our diplomatic people have advance assurances that Kim won't make a fuss over the issue."

"Flipping is one of Kim's diplomatic ploys. If he flips his position on this he'll look like outraged innocence and make us look less than serious about negotiation. Flipping on any issue, even those you think were tentatively agreed upon early on, is a typical gaming ploy they use all the time. Expect it and ignore it and get on with your own agenda."

"Why would they do a thing like that," Bolton asked.

"Because Kim is a staller and a gamester, like his father and grandfather," Callahan replied.

"Mr. President," Pompeo said, "maybe we should raise that issue with our diplomatic staff. I'm sure sorry we lost our career Korean

< 36 >

expert Joe Yun. He just retired in February and we don't have an experienced replacement."

"Maybe you are better off," Charlie responded. "Some of these career diplomats might be part of the problem and not the solution, especially if they are rigid protocolists or believers that only diplomacy that crawls along at a snail's pace is true diplomacy."

"Handle it, Mike," said the president. "This has been a heavy discussion gentlemen. Mike, I think it is time to move to our next destination."

As the entourage filed out of the room, Carlos had the thought that this president was probably giving the Secret Service staff the biggest workout they had in years. He was like the legendary perpetual motion machine. However impressive history might find these efforts, history was mainly interested in results and outcomes. Time was the necessary ingredient now. Would they make the same old mistakes? Would they make new ones? Or would they get it right this time? What was right, anyway?

"Hey Lobo! Come out of your trance," Callahan said.

"Si, my jefe," replied Carlos.

< 37 >

8

DELILAH AND THE FAIRIES

As the president's party exited the room, a messenger came to speak to General Callahan, pulling him out of the room. This left Carlos, Choe and Charlie alone with the lovely Delilah Cummings. She had stayed behind because she would be working with them. It had all happened so fast.

As they chatted it became clear Delilah could handle herself well in a room of slightly awed gentlemen, even those less well-behaved than this bunch. They noticed she had some executive skills and smarts when she asked what other ideas they had for achieving the goal of finding the hidden bases in North Korea. Her next question came as a surprise.

"So," Delilah said, addressing Carlos and Choe, "Are you guys fairies or what? I would just like to know so we can get on okay together."

Choe rattled off something in rapid Korean, "Is she crazy? We are human beings, not fairies."

Carlos responded in Korean, "Fairy is a term to describe homosexuals, Choe. It's American slang."

Choe laughed. "I must learn more of your slang. I was thinking of Tinkerbell in Peter Pan."

Carlos looked at Delilah and responded to her question. "No, Choe and I are not, but I can't speak for Charles. I've only known him two weeks, but Choe and I have been pals for six years."

"Not!" said Charlie.

"Why do you ask? Are you a lesbian?" Carlos asked.

"No," she replied. "Forgive me if I offended you with my abruptness. I'm not used to seeing men who work with each other who are not competing with each other. It is a new and refreshing change to what I'm used to. Maybe it's a class thing."

Carlos thought that if he had been gay, contact with Delilah might have tempted him to change his sexual affiliation. To which he

< 38 >

knew his homosexual friends would say, "Yech!" We are what we are, he thought laughingly.

Choe smiled and said, "Ms. Cummings, since we are being candid, I have a question for you, which of course you don't have to answer, but how did you come to be Mr. Pompeo's special assistant?"

Delilah smiled good-naturedly. "Don't worry about me, sweetie, I'm no #MeToo girl. My daddy made a BIG contribution to the president's campaign…and besides, my daddy wants me out from underfoot and have something to keep me busy. He says, 'An idle mind is the devil's workshop.'"

"Caramba," Carlos said, "there are still people that talk that way? My grandfather used to say that. And the village priest at Pojoaque where I grew up."

Choe was again stumped by American slang, and it showed on his face. Koreans have little truck with devils, but they get forest and mountain spirits.

"So, Delilah, let's get down to work since there's a lot to do and you're going to be in charge," Carlos said. "But first, let me call our sandwich service and get a selection of lunch goodies up here."

For the next three hours they talked seriously. Delilah was absorbing the information and discussion like a massive human sponge and appeared to be processing the input quickly.

Charlie, most of all, was in awe of the Big D. He had never come across a woman as smart as himself, and maybe brainier. He knew this by the questions she asked. Only time would tell if she could turn intelligence into results. He knew few people who could.

They decided that although their operation was supposed to be, by bureaucratic rules, 'top secret' they would be open about their goals, but not on how they planned to achieve them. They would be using a disinformation routine. It was useful that the North Koreans, and others like the Chinese and Russians, got wind of the enterprise. Ostensibly, they would use traditional methods such as direct "facility" searches in official records and trading intel (spook gossip) with other "spy" agencies. Also, they would plant hints that they were trying to work a "mole" into the North Korean military. This would escalate North Korea's paranoia.

Their real methodology was multi-pronged and totally unconventional. First, there was Choe's "pamphlet and gold coin" idea aimed at increasing defector information on secret nuke/ICBM

< 39 >

facilities. A variant of this was Charlie's suggestion that they should offer fifty gold coins for an up-to-date North Korean facilities manual.

Second, their geographer/cartographer would be looking at remote mountain locations, comparing current North Korean maps with late 19th century and early 20th century maps. The belief was facilities were being hidden by "being dropped from the maps." The facilities and infrastructure and connecting roads thus deleted were likely evidence of hidden secret bases.

Third, Carlos believed that the North Koreans just had to have a hidden base on Mount Paektu, the highest mountain in Korea at 2,749 meters, and a place considered sacred in their cultural history. It was also known as Paekdusan and had recently been converted to a mountain resort, tourist showcase. It was easily reachable to many South Koreans who accessed it through air flights from major cities in China. Since it lay right on the border with China, a South Korea tourist can also come within one foot of North Korea by taking a sightseeing launch boat trip from China.

Another possibility he considered that could hide a launch site was Mount Kumgang in the Marble Mountains preserve in the extreme southeast part of North Korea.

Back in 1995 or so, a South Korean housewife who wandered off the trail there was shot dead, ending tourist interest in this lovely area.

Why would Carlos think there might be a hidden base on Mount Paektu? Because of the Koreans' long historic belief in "geomancy," which was called "Feng Shui" by the Chinese. It was a difficult concept to explain to Westerners. Some places were right or more 'in' than others. The most powerful mountain spirits were supposed to live on Mount Paektu. Carlos was betting on this traditionalism. Pyongyang was traditionally high in geomancy/Feng Shui.

The fourth idea was that a geologist should be hired to find North Korea's most outstanding Karst formations where limestone caves abound. These natural caves carved by Mother Nature would most likely be the sites for hidden installations.

< 40 >

9

THE FOUR MUSKETEERS

As their three-hour marathon meeting started running out of steam, General Callahan put it to bed and set a reconvene time for the next day at ten a.m.

"So, Delilah, can we three musketeers escort you home?" Carlos asked. "If you don't mind slumming we can get you home by hopping on the Metro first."

"I would love the opportunity to see plain folk instead of our chauffeur Michael, though he is a nice man. In return, it is likely you'll get an invitation to dinner if Daddy's day hasn't been too awful."

Charlie smiled, "Let's go then, we are now four musketeers. Two of these gents are martial artists of the first caliber and this, my cane, has hidden talents."

"Charlie is an Olympic-class fencer," Choe explained.

"Yipes! said the lovely Delilah. "That must be one of those devilish sword-canes I've read about."

"Vamoose amigos and amiga, it's time to mosey along," Carlos said. Am I talking Spanglish, he wondered.

Mr. Cummings knew his daughter, Delilah, was attracted to men but what the devil was she doing with three of them at the door, he wondered.

"Daddy, these are some of the people at the Pentagon that I'll be working with. They're all doctors, can you imagine? Any one of them would make a great husband for Valerie."

"Doctors? Medical doctors?"

"No silly. They are historians, and athletes too."

"Well now, that sounds interesting. Would you gentlemen care to stay for dinner?"

The three men looked at each other and nodded their heads simultaneously, and that was before they saw Valerie.

< 41 >

Delilah smiled to herself as her father walked her guests to the library for pre-dinner libations. She knew Valerie would be making her "princess" entry soon, exuding pheromones and coyness. Within ten minutes she would find out from the servants what was happening, then swiftly make her move. She would have made a great field marshal, if they ever let women lead armies. When they were younger they had competed for boys and then men. It had been fun but it was all silly. The kind of people you could easily sway were not the kind of people she was interested in now, Delilah thought.

They all got better acquainted over dinner. Early in their chit-chat Delilah whispered to her sister, "Close your mouth Val, you're absolutely gawking at Charlie."

Delilah looked up and saw Carlos, who was seated at the far side of the table, smile broadly. Why is he smiling? Delilah wondered, he couldn't possibly have heard me.

Delilah noticed after the first half hour had passed since Valerie's entrance the interest shown by her three gentlemen associates had waned in its intensity. These guys were not too susceptible to flash and glamour. Her opinion of them rose, especially when they left early. It was after all a work night and these were serious guys, not playboy types.

A few minutes after they left, Delilah got a call from Mike Pompeo.

"How did it work out Ms. Cummings?"

"Great, Mike! They are a good bunch and I think we can contribute something valuable. Thanks for the opportunity."

"Well, good. You're on your own now kid. You don't need to check in at all with me anymore. If you have any questions about how many people you can hire or whatever else comes up, talk to that Mr. Mortimer I told you about. And say hello to your daddy for me."

"Will do. Thanks again Uncle Mike." He wasn't actually her uncle but it set the right tone for their relationship; this was a town of wagging tongues and wolf ears.

May 1, 2018
The Pentagon

The following morning the three musketeers, coffee cups in hand, met with General Callahan at nine.

< 42 >

"We survived our first big pow-wow with the big chiefs," Choe said.

"Well-done braves," said General Callahan.

"You know, Carlos," Charlie said, "if we pass along that 'Afghanistan Bananastand' warning to Bolton or the president, they might use the opportunity to implement their own 'first strike' option."

"Of course I thought of that ahead of time. I'm not bothered by it because the likelihood of that happening is very slight. You know the four of us in this room are small potatoes and are not going to be in the loop that orders a first strike, but by telling these big guys when we think the North Koreans are ready to blow, we are giving the president the advance warning needed to prepare our military for what's coming.

"Also, we've told them that China and Russia are not likely to allow us to implement the Bolton first strike plan because that could precipitate World War III. Even though China and Russia's goals have changed since the Korean War of nineteen fifty, they were still allies of North Korea back then. Nations, like individual people, find it hard to just walk away from old friends.

"What could change their minds is finding out that North Korea has nukes aimed at Moscow and Beijing. I suspect they do because in their paranoia they trust nobody."

"Not only that," Choe added, "with our warning, the president could put our forces on standby and wait for the North Koreans to fire first. That's a political positive we'll need, especially if something goes bad and it easily could if we don't find those hidden bases ahead of time."

"Isn't all this rather Machiavellian, Carlos?" Charlie asked.

"You're right, Charlie," Carlos agreed, "but I'm beginning to have an intuition that Bolton's first strike plan is the only one that has a chance of getting the job done right. But yes, our top team is not into playing deep games; they all seem too straightforward. But I agree with Choe's feeling that if the second Korean War started there in Korea it would be nice if they started it, because we will surely have to finish it no matter what the cost to us."

"Gentleman," General Callahan said, "we have to do some brainstorming on the Sanction E assignment we were given but we will table that for a while. We need to help Ms. Cummings launch her project first because that will take time to bear fruit for us. Did you gentlemen get Ms. Delilah Cummings home safely last night?"

< 43 >

"Sure did, General," Carlos replied as the other two men nodded enthusiastically. "We got invited to dinner too. What a feed. We were three bachelors in hog heaven! What a cook they have."

"By the way, General, who is her father?" Charlie asked.

"Don't know him. Obviously, someone politically potent."

"I know who he is, General," Choe said. "Read about him in *Forbes* or the *Wall Street Journal* or somewhere. They call him the Lazarus Man because he revives dead or dying companies."

"Looks like Delilah may have some of her father's talent," Charlie said.

"Let's hope so. Straighten your ties guys, I hear her coming down the hall now," Carlos warned.

Three seconds later there was a knock on the door. Charlie gave Carlos a very respectful smile.

< 44 >

10

The FBI Knocks, Carlos Doesn't Answer

May 1, 2018
The Pentagon/3:00 p.m.

Carlos, Choe, and Delilah were deep into a last-minute planning session for their upcoming sojourn to South Korea. A secretary that Carlos had never seen before walked up to him and said, "Two FBI agents are here to speak with you."

"Probably about that incident with the president," Delilah said.

Carlos looked at the young lady and said, "Tell them I'm too busy to see them today. They need to call first. Also, tell them I can't see them for two other reasons: First, it's May Day, and second, my horoscope caster said it was a bad day to talk to strangers. Tell them they are welcome to send me a zucchini if they wish but I have nothing to tell them."

As the confused secretary walked away, Carlos said, "To think I idolized these guys when I was a kid!"

"Bravo Carlos," Choe said. "No one who talks with the FBI comes away without mud on their face or reputations. These guys have become political hatchet men. They are untrustworthy and biased, and place politics over objectivity."

< 45 >

11

Holiday in Seoul

May 3, 2018
Airport/Seoul, South Korea

As Choe, Carlos, and Delilah cleared Customs they were met by three men. The older man was Choe's father and the others were security guards. Choe hugged his father, then the old man hugged Carlos and said, "Welcome son number two, and Delilah 'friend of my sons.'"

When Delilah took the reins of her presidential assignment she had moved into high gear. She urgently wanted to establish a base here in South Korea for the intelligence gathering plan (gold coins for information). She had interviewed candidates by phone and Skype but wanted to meet them in person.

Choe and Carlos wanted to lay their hands on old maps and current maps of North Korea so they decided to do a joint foray together.

Their first joint endeavor was interviewing candidates for the 'intelligence bureau' here. As everyone who has done this kind of work knows, that's a hairy task. People are not always what they say on paper or computer disk. Delilah grilled people mercilessly, pushing them to disclose themselves, their experiences, their backgrounds, and even their opinions.

After a quick break for a late working lunch, Delilah turned to Choe and Carlos and said, "If you have any comments before I hire, let me know. I've decided to hire this Francie Sansin as director and this 'Red Hand' guy as her assistant. What do you think?"

Carlos and Choe smiled at each other and nodded.

Choe spoke first, "This Francie person is one of the smartest ladies and best chess player in all of South Korea. 'Red Hand' has a good reputation in the community. He defected from the north ten years ago. He is loyal and a man of multiple talents."

< 46 >

"Why the smiles, guys? Do you know these people?"

"Sure," replied Choe. "Francie is my little sister. My full name is Choe Yi Sansin, but I like just Choe Yi."

"We didn't want to influence you in any way," Carlos told her, "so no charges of nepotism could be raised in the future."

"Thanks. You guys really are gentlemen."

The three exhausted travelers spent the night at Choe's parents' house and were allowed to sleep late the next day.

Francie accompanied the traveling trio the next day so she and Delilah could get better acquainted. Francie was short and slim, black-haired and plain. She was hyperactive with large eyes which made her look owlish if she was thinking or hawkish if she was pissed off. Choe's nickname for her was "The Walking Brain."

Their first group visit was to the special collections branch of the Seoul Library where Dr. Numantia of Stanford University took delivery on a long-term loan of historic 19th and 20th century map books for use with his Korean economic studies.

Next, they visited Red Hand and asked for his company the rest of the day. Red Hand was larger and more muscular than most South Koreans and physically agile. He was reasonably smart and adaptable. He had lived through hell and had landed on his feet. He was dependable and likable.

They told him of their need for a modern map atlas of North Korea. They accompanied him while he visited some shops and made some cellular calls. After two hours, he reported that no one in town had one and he would have to track down Black Hand a locally famous character who was a notorious Secret Army trader/buyer; a blockade runner/swapper who eluded economic sanctions placed on North Korea by the West and China. To North Korean officials he was a patriot. To North Korean peasants he was Robin Hood. To fellow merchants he was an okay guy because he kept his word.

He wasn't notorious for being bad or double-dealing but because he only took on jobs he liked and worked on his own timetable. He was often out of touch for days for planned drinking and debauchery where he recirculated coin in the world economy. Why was he called Black Hand? Simply because he worked in the Black Market economy and needed a nifty moniker to impress people with his ninja skills and create an image.

Luckily, they found Black Hand totally sober in his small hovel,

< 47 >

contemplating dinner with only a few tiny coins in his pocket. Black Hand and Red Hand were clearly twins. Red Hand adopted his *nom de guerre* because of a permanent red scar on his right hand. Their other differences were small. Black Hand had several visible knife scars on his face and arms testifying to his real, tough life experiences. Where Red was sober and serious, Black was happy go lucky and independent.

"Ask him to dinner, Red, our treat," Delilah said.

The two men hugged each other like long lost brothers, which is exactly what they were. They knew every reunion could be their last.

By the end of the evening they were well acquainted with Black Hand, who was a likable and interesting scoundrel. As they left him back at his hovel, Choe handed him a wad of money for Delilah to "start him on his way tomorrow." Francie was to handle plane tickets for Pyongyang tomorrow if he so chose. She was now his official contact and the two shook hands solemnly. They were in business.

< 48 >

12

THE GORDIAN KNOT AND THE TRIUMVIRATE

Long, long ago, Gordius of Phrygia was a noted Necromancer and Gamemaster. His most famous trick was tying a knot so fantastically complicated no one could untie it. According to an oracle, whoever could do it would become Master of Asia. Many tried, all failed. Alexander came by to try his hand (actually two) at the chore. Alex figured out Gord's gig right away so he pulled out his sword and hacked open the knot. The rest is history. Learn.

May 15, 2018
The Cassandra Group Confers with the Triumvirate

"General Callahan," said the president, "does the Cassandra Group have any idea how we can force Kim's hand and denuclearize the Korean Peninsula without having to blow North Korea to Kingdom Come first, as John wants us to do?"

"We're not sure, but we have hashed things around and come up with a goofy idea, it's the Sanction E that John requested in the last meeting. We borrowed this idea from our judicial branch, from divorce court specifically. It is simply joint custody. When a family breaks up and both responsible parents want custody of a child, this joint custody comes into play. In this case of course, Kim's 'children' are his nuke and ICBM launch facilities and his chemical/bio warfare facilities.

"So, for this plan you need to convince Kim that he should let our scientists and soldiers into all of these facilities so we may jointly take possession and operate the facilities along with his people, holding them in trust for the future until the time North and South Korea reconcile. The fate of these facilities will be determined at that time by all the parties concerned. Only then will Japan and China and other countries feel free to commit serious financial investment resources in North Korean development. It is a viable way Kim can fulfill his

< 49 >

overdue promises of prosperity to his undernourished people.

"Of course, as part of 'takeover procedures' the settings on the launch devices at all sites should be erased or set at zero under joint U.S. and North Korean scientific supervision. We are, of course, interested in recording what settings were there first. Our hunch is one of those settings is targeting Beijing and possibly Moscow, so we should have, whenever possible, a Chinese and Russian representative on the inspection/takeover teams.

"This is a risky and grandiose plan but it just might appeal to the strange mind of your 'Rocket Man.' It would allow him to save some face, and his life. He needs to know that any attempt to take total control of any of these joint sites will not be met by negotiation, but by immediate obliteration. Even if we have to kill our own people, we must not allow hostages to be taken. He must believe we will do what we say, so instant automatic retaliation must be built into that plan.

"You understand that this 'convincing' of Kim is not something to be leisurely negotiated at 'diplomatic pace' over months or years as has been allowed in the past. Give him sixty days to take it or leave it.

"If he agrees, and signs, he must open one of his sites every three weeks, starting in Nyongbyon, and another three weeks later, and so on, until all are under joint custody. He must provide a comprehensive site inventory list within sixty days of the agreement. This 'generous' extra time period for the site inventory list is to let maximum political pressure build up for complete disclosure. Unreported sites would be a critical future danger to us all.

"Also, the discovery by us of an unreported launch site must be held over their heads as a serious violation of the treaty which will reactivate expired economic sanctions immediately."

Mike Pompeo was the first to react, "Wow! You guys may have something there. We have got to talk that idea over. What do you think, John?"

"Very interesting. It just might be strange enough to appeal to Kim."

"It would require a lot of salesmanship to pitch this idea," Choe said.

"The diplomats will hate it," Charlie interjected, "and it will impugn the president's sanity again, and of course our own."

"If you can sell this proposition," Carlos said, "you can sell iceboxes to Eskimos, and save a lot of bloodshed. Maybe another

< 50 >

Gordian knot will be cut and get the president his deserved laurel wreath after all."

"Carlos means the president might someday get a Nobel Peace Prize after all, not one dangled under his nose by diplomats or bureaucrats to make him go soft in negotiations, but one earned by achievement," Choe said.

"I can't help thinking he deserves one of those even if he uses Sanction A. Somehow my subconscious mind is telling me that, but I can't consciously figure why that is so," Carlos said. "Maybe modern man is getting too rational and leaving our instincts behind, which could be an evolutionary mistake."

"You're getting too deep for me, son," Mr. Pompeo said.

"Carlos is too deep for most people, sir," said General Callahan, "but now we need to show you the 'F' plan. It's a variant of 'E' but instead of jointly running the facilities with North Korea we would use on-site sophisticated monitoring devices twenty-four seven backed up by a small army of our own monitors, inspectors, and guards living on-site or nearby at our own facilities. The North Koreans would still operate and control the facility, however.

"We think we can still get plenty of qualified rocket engineers from the Ukraine, from the closing of the great Yuzhmash missile factory there. This is a beefed-up version of what didn't work before. To offset the placing of our people on North Korean soil we could offer to pull out some of our troops in South Korea. Any security breaches by North Korea could be set up to automatically reinstate economic sanctions.

"The primary focus of the inspections would be to see that no payload launch vehicles are 're-targeted' to anywhere or are ever activated. You might see these monitors or inspectors as modern descendants of Paul Revere and his riders who warned, 'The British are coming!' Now they might say, 'The missiles are coming!'"

"This idea I think I like," said the president.

"We're just now sending around the table some simple writeups of all these proposals for you so you can study the various options," General Callahan said.

"I think our friend, Mr. Moon, is getting too deep into this peace and reconciliation thing," the president said. "I think he wants it too much."

"Well, maybe he wants to be known as the 'Great Reconciliator'

< 51 >

but fame is fleeting," Bolton replied.

"So is the fickle finger of fate," Callahan added. "Eventually we'll learn what direction it's pointing."

The president stood up and the meeting was over.

< 52 >

13

LOOKING FOR THE HIDDEN, WITH CIA HELP

May 28, 2018
The Pentagon

Delilah Cummings' work group, dubbed by Choe as "The Searchers," quickly discovered Karst formations in two interesting mountains that were 90km apart, and in twelve other locations as well. A geologist had been consulted first and a world expert on cave spelunking provided useful information as well.

The first mountain was Paekdu or Paekdusan. Choe and Carlos were eager to check it out but decided that reconnaissance in a developed tourist area required special planning. Maybe a standard tourist trip first to get the feel of the area would be best. They thought they might do the same for Mt. Kumgang in the Marble Mountains.

The second 'karst' mountain they considered had no name on either old maps or new. Because it was 40km northeast of Hyesan, a major city near the Chinese border, they dubbed it Mount Hyesan.

Mount Hyesan was a good candidate to hide a secret installation. It had a flat saddle not far from the summit. Nearby, old maps had indicated an unpaved road and current maps showed nothing there, not even a trail. Carlos and Choe were very excited about it. The question was how they could find out what was in that mountain. They had contacted the CIA and given geo coordinates to have the area watched twenty-four seven to see if any airplane or helicopter activity had been noted by satellite day image, infrared or truck traffic along the supposedly abandoned road leading there.

They hit the jackpot the first night when helicopter and truck traffic were spotted. The CIA was very interested.

The entire Cassandra Group was meeting with Delilah's Searchers to discuss a way they could find out more. A young CIA

< 53 >

agent, Mark Canfield, a gadget kind of fellow, was also present. Mark was of medium height, black haired, and kind of nondescript-looking, but he was a sharp dresser.

Choe and Carlos had cooked up a crazy plan and pitched it to the combined groups. Choe started it off by saying, "My family has relatives in the north 60km southwest from Mount Paektu. We will try to make a deal with one of Kim's 'Secret Army' people (modern blockade runners like Clark Gable in *Gone with the Wind* but not as handsome) to deliver some non-perishable foodstuffs to our family there, as part of an agreement to deliver food to other local North Koreans who were always eager to do business on the Black Market, since continual sanctions pinched their regular suppliers of goods from the West. We will be using this Black Hand fellow we met recently in South Korea, especially since he was born in Hyesan."

"Choe," said Delilah, "what foods will you be shipping them?"

"Spam and Velveeta Cheese. My father's in shipping and marketing."

"Sounds like a good choice. That would be a valuable cargo."

"It would, and we'll be taking along one of my father's trusted guards to protect it, Carlos and me. We think Black Hand will leave us alone and play it straight. His brother says he's not really political but likes to live free and play Robin Hood sometimes."

"After making a drop shipment to Choe's family," Carlos said, "Black Hand will take us to his village to drop off the major part of the shipment. From there we go to Mount Hyesan to climb the mountain. We are real life mountain climbers, you know. At the same time, we will photograph Mount Hyesan for a new book we're writing entitled, *Mountains of North Korea*.

"When we get near the top where the Karst cavern is, we will launch a small commercial drone, if we can figure out how to get a camera on it. That's where we were hoping to get CIA help."

"I can help with that," Mark said, "assuming my boss agrees. I think you also need someone else on your team because your plan is a bit top heavy. I'm a practiced photographer too. Done some hiking but not technical stuff. You know, a venture like this is really dangerous. Can you guys handle firearms? You need to be carrying openly. Something like personal pistols not heavier weaponry, as that would brand you as a troublemaker."

< 54 >

"Choe and I have grown up around guns and we've taken formal instruction as well," replied Carlos.

"And watched how Marshal Rooster Cogburn did it," laughed Choe.

"And 'Little Big Man' the Indian gunfighter," added Carlos.

"What about the publishers for that mountain book," asked Delilah, "will that be a real cover for you? Have you actually talked to anyone?"

"No, but we've got good counterfeit credentials from *National Geographic Magazine*," Choe replied.

"These 'Secret Army' guys have a strong survival instinct. If Mark comes with us he's got to project a lot of 'nerd' persona to mask his CIA identity."

"General Callahan," said Delilah, "are you willing to let Carlos and Choe go on this dangerous undertaking? We might lose them both and I, for one, would be devastated."

"Delilah," Callahan replied, "I feel the same as you. I'm not happy to let them go as they're both like sons to me, but you can't protect even your own sons sometimes. We discussed this extensively and they really want to do something positive for the future of Korea. Young men have so few chances to do anything exciting or useful these days."

"When you lovable lugs get back I'll talk my Daddy into throwing a reunion wingding for you."

Carlos and Choe gave her a thumbs up sign.

The new recruits of Delilah's "Searchers" group, even the old Ukrainian rocket scientist Dr. Kuznosko, who had worked at Yuzhmash in the Ukraine, knew there were subliminal messages going to and fro. These young people, he thought to himself.

< 55 >

14

The Cassandra Group Meets Alone

May 31, 2018

The big pow-wow between the President of the United States and Kim Jong Un was less than two weeks away. The on-again/off-again meeting in Singapore looked like it was going to happen. The presidential in-group of three was now augmented to four with the inclusion of Gina Haspel, newly appointed head of the CIA.

The Cassandra Group's input had not been sought since that last dramatic meeting of May 15, however, they had not been entirely forgotten. As requested, General Callahan's security rating had been upped and the CIA had come through with a copy of currently known North Korean launch sites which would help with the unmasking of hidden North Korea sites.

"So General," said Carlos, "you've heard the president and Mike Pompeo talking about 'rapid denuclearization,' do you think that means they got the messages we were transmitting at our last meeting?"

"Possibly, Carlos. In this business you seldom know if the big-wigs are understanding your spiel so you have to keep pitching and not get worried about the score. Remember the Cassandra Legend. Cassandra's prophecies were true, but nobody believed them. We are often in the same circumstance. We make predictions based on what historians before us said happened in the past and based on our own best judgments of the various optimum options available to our leaders and customers. Our leaders frequently ignore or misunderstand our advice and do something dumb or stupid. Just accept it, and like Odysseus, disregard all Gods or men in your way and go home to where you want to be. Another way to look at it is we don't so much give them ready-made solutions to problems as help them clarify their thinking."

"Great pep talk, General," Choe said.

< 56 >

"Nice oratory, sir," added Charlie. "That did clarify some things for me.

"I'm pretty sure," said Callahan, "that Mike and the president are also reacting to the cautions of the diplomats and that denuclearization expert, Sigfried Hecker, your fellow professor at Stanford, who is talking about the technical aspects and fine points of the process and telling everyone that it's going to take all of fifteen years at least to denuclearize."

"Meantime," said Charlie, "the North Koreans are happy as clams to have this old guy feted because it helps with their strategy of extending things out as long as they can and giving as little as they can. No wonder he's always been welcome at Yongbyon."

Choe laughed. "Not only is denuclearization his 'baby' but he wrote a book about it with the help of a couple assistants. Book writing intellectuals are no better at knowing they're being used than anyone else."

"You know though," Charlie said, "about that other prof at Stanford who has written articles favorable to the president and even called him a slasher of Gordian political knots. Hanson is his name, I think, Victor David Hanson. Per his opinion, the president has already initially slashed the diplomatic Gordian knot of always treating Kim with kid gloves, by calling him 'Rocket Man' and threatening him back and using the same blunt tactics on him that he has been using on us."

"Some say the president is no ideologue but a problem solver," said Carlos, "but I would add that he relies on his instincts rather than the bureaucracy as other presidents have."

"I think," Callahan said, "that he's telling people the June twelfth meeting will be a 'get acquainted' meeting to tamp down unrealistic expectations for the summit. A first day breakthrough is possible but not likely. Maybe they'll sign a piece of paper that will make political happy news, or at least a declaration of intent."

"It may take a couple of meetings before they begin real negotiations," Choe added.

"Unless Kim decides to withdraw from negotiations because of cold feet," Charlie said. Then you would have what you Americans call a Mexican standoff where neither side can make an effective move and you're right back where you were before. But worse, since some of his nukes might be able to hit some of our cities if he ever went rogue-crazy. Kim talks tough but he's really hiding behind China and

< 57 >

Russia's skirts, a comfortable place from which to issue his threats."

"In the meantime," Carlos added, "all this recent fuss over 'maximum effort' was just a useful way for the Super Hawks to make a political statement to the president and try and hobble his negotiating stance. In short, good old-fashioned American meddling and disinformation, like Madison Avenue, the media, the government and assorted nuisances all Americans are subjected to twenty-four seven from the day they're born. It's amazing that most of us grow up reasonably sane and develop very solid mental shields against bullshit. To think a Russian troll (human or supernatural) could really influence our choice of president is wishful-thinking fantasy.

"As Amelia Peabody said in her last novel, *The Painted Queen*, 'We all mess with peoples' minds every day, Emerson. We seek to influence them with words and acts of varying effectiveness. Some methods are more effective than others.'"

"Bravo!" said Choe. "That needed to be said. It's hard to work for a president who is constantly being threatened with impeachment by the political opposition and being called a traitor because he is trying to normalize the United States' relationship with the second-most powerful nation on the planet. This level of hysterical and irrational resistance has never happened before in your history. It's happened in South Korea history, but it's not pleasant to recall."

"Gentlemen," Callahan said, "it's time to change topics. How is Delilah's searchers group coming along?"

"Very well," replied Charlie. "Delilah hired two Koreans to run the program to pick up leads on hidden bases. Francie is the brain and treasurer for gold coins and Red Hand is her right-hand man. He is a North Korean defector who used to be a government messenger so he's real familiar with hundreds of places he's been in North Korea."

Charlie continued, "They interview supposed defectors or information peddlers very carefully. They Google sites if they can, consult maps, current and old, all before Francie approves payment. Lots of people, desperate for money, make up bogus stories. They also have their share of government agents, mostly North Koreans, but some South Koreans and Chinese. They've picked up accurate information on three sites that the CIA has confirmed are hidden military sites of unknown function.

"Francie set up a physical message board and a computer one so families looking for someone could have a way to connect. She also

< 58 >

provides refreshments for the people who spend time there. It's sort of like a social center."

"By the way," Choe interjects, "Francie is my little sister. The family calls her 'Super Brain.'"

"Choe, I didn't know that," Charlie said. "I doubt that Delilah did either."

General Callahan raises his coffee cup, "I propose a toast to our Francie Brigade Affiliate in Seoul."

Everyone clinks their cups together and cheers.

General Callahan smiles and looks to Carlos, Choe and Charlie. "Are you guys still getting dinner invites at the Cummings house?"

Carlos replied, "Por cierto, mi General. Who could turn down the combination of beautiful women, superb cooking and lovely surroundings."

"Actually," said Charlie, blushing, "we have an open invite for dinner every Friday, unless someone is out of town."

"Choe has finally found a chess partner who is in his league," Carlos said. "Mr. Cummings is a terror on the chessboard, and believe it or not, a jokester. He told Choe last time that the last person he played chess with had died of a heart attack because Cummings had opened with the famous 'Lost Van Goom's Gambit.' He then said his daughters chided him because his opponent had also been one of their suitors. When Choe got the jokes he nearly knocked over the chess pieces from laughing. Then Mr. Cummings described his daughters when they were small as 'easy on the eyes but hard on the ears.'"

Everyone enjoyed a good laugh, then Choe added, "At the same gathering, Carlos was helping Delilah with a jigsaw puzzle and we saw them, holding the same puzzle piece and staring into each other's eyes like they were both 'Moonstruck.'"

Carlos said, "You're right, Choe, I was nearly 'Lost in Space' that day, but I've decided that romantic entanglements at work can get too sticky and having two girlfriends at the same time is dangerous."

Hearing this, Charlie's eyes grew as large as saucers, and he smiled like a blushing Cheshire cat.

"Let's call it a day, gentlemen," said General Callahan.

< 59 >

15

THE BIG DAY

June 12, 2018/5:00 p.m.

The president met with Kim Jong Un today and they buddied up and signed a piece of paper, a sort of declaration of intent to negotiate. The press and the president's detractors (he has more of those than Rome had slaves) agreed he had not made a maximum effort (whatever the hell that means).

The man on the street and the stock market were happy that the president and 'Rocket Man' were no longer trading boasts, barbs or bombs.

"So, Carlos," General Callahan said, "what do you think about the president's decision to stop joint U.S. and South Korean military maneuvers and exercises?"

"From a military point of view it makes good sense. These 'war games,' and I accept that graphic term, were a rehearsal for recreating yesterday's Korean War. It's like the French tinkering with the Maginot Line while German Panzer drivers were being issued road maps end-running the supposedly unbreakable line. Any war fought today will be mostly over in a few hours with missiles, ICBMs, and jet aircraft, though the cleanup would take the infantry months more if we wanted to commit to such a task. In the meantime, most of our troops over there can come home. Ask them how they feel about that."

Carlos continued, "From a diplomatic point of view another message is being sent. Seems like the president wants the South Koreans to assume more of their own defense. That seems to be his message in Europe too, to NATO, and in particular to Germany, to fund more of their own defense and cease relying on American taxpayers to do it for them."

Choe and Charlie nodded their heads in agreement.

"Looks like we're unanimous on that one," General Callahan agreed.

< 60 >

Choe laughed. "Nobody is sneakier at funding than the North Koreans. The North Korean currency, the 'won,' trades at eight thousand to one U.S. dollar on the open market. The won is also artificially inflated by the government in transactions involving foreign currency and is thus economic extortion to foreigners who do business there."

Choe continued, "The worst extortion was done by Kim's father in 2009 when the government erased all the North Koreans' personal savings by changing the old currency for new at a rate of one 'new' for a hundred 'old.' Then he blamed one of his finance ministers for this 'accident.' Hah!"

Carlos interjected, "I understand Franco did the same thing when he took over, but he only stole one-half of peoples' savings, not ninety-nine percent."

Choe laughed. "Kim recently used the same excuse his father had modeled by blaming reclamation officials for not building hydro facilities on time when he knew they couldn't because the water was being used to turn Kim's nuclear reactor turbines to make atomic bombs. Apparently, the 'Big Lie' still works."

< 61 >

16

STRANGE DOINGS AT THE RED DRAGON

June 16, 2018/8:00 p.m.
The Red Dragon Restaurant, Washington, DC

Sally kissed Carlos on the forehead. "You're very worried about something Carlitos, what is it? Digame."

"Witch," he murmured, laughingly. "You can read minds. And you understand Spanish."
Choe and Charlie smirked while Darlene, the new hardworking cartographer of Delilah's searcher group, was puzzled. Darlene was being treated to her first dinner at the infamous Red Dragon. She didn't know any of the others very well but she was amazed and amused. Darlene wasn't a denizen of the swamp; she hailed from flattest Kansas.

"I started today to make the final arrangements for our trip with Mark but I sort of froze up," Carlos told the group. "I had a feeling that something was wrong but I'm not sure what."

"Oh! Oh!" Sally said. "Sounds like your unconscious is trying to deliver a message. Better listen because we know your unconscious is really good at delivering you messages that matter."

Carlos sat silently thinking as Charlie, tonight's designated order-person rattled off the selections to the waiter.

"You're right, Sally," Carlos said before he gave her a sloppy kiss on the lips. "Us dumb cowboys have been trying to take over Mike's job and do it ourselves. What we need to do is better prepare him to do it himself by giving him the pointers he needs to sharpen up his act. That will lower the danger level all around. We pick the sites and his guys explore them at their own risk. We need to get him deeply bonded to Black Hand."

Darlene sat, quietly listening, with her mouth open. She thought to herself, what are these people talking? Are they spies or something?

< 62 >

She knew little about her central part in this jigsaw puzzle drama. She was the cartographer who had discovered Mount Hyesan. She was also an unknowing focal point.

She would certainly have lots of gossip to tell Delilah on Monday. It was Delilah who encouraged her to accept the invitation from these three, interesting, brainy guys to go to the Red Dragon in the first place. They simultaneously attracted and upset her. Darlene thought Sally was the most beautiful woman she had ever met, maybe even prettier than her boss. It was a close horse race.

June 18, 2018/9:30 a.m.
The Pentagon Conference Room

"Morning Delilah," Choe said as he intercepted her entering the empty conference room. "You're early you know, doesn't start til ten."

I wanted to talk to you before the meeting, Choe. Can you tell me why Carlos has suddenly turned cool towards me? Is it true he has a girlfriend?"

"Sure, but next time you should ask Carlos directly. It's kind of like a timing thing. He met Sally shortly before he met you. He likes you both but he's no 'two-timer' so Sally's his girlfriend and he wants you to be his friend. Carlos is really old-fashioned you know; Spanish people are often like that."

"I see," Delilah said.

"Probably you don't. I know you are just saying that. You need to go with us Saturday night to the Red Dragon and meet Sally for yourself. I promise you it won't be Saturday Night Fever or Big Trouble in Little China. Meet Sally and then you'll see. No one will mind your coming. On the contrary, all would be pleased to see you there. By the way, your American slang is not only picturesque but very targeted in meaning. Carlos explained to me what a two-timer is."

"Wow," Delilah replied, "lots to think about. Maybe I should come dressed as Wonder Woman."

"Come dressed as you please. Your friends know you're Wonder Woman."

"Choe, you're such a charmer."

"So, are we all still welcome Friday nights at your place?"

"Of course."

"How is Val doing?"

< 63 >

"Choe, Val is really young and she's infatuated with you, or maybe Charlie, or maybe both of you. She's switching her major to history for next year. Be gentle with her and give her a chance to grow up."

"We will, Big Sister. I'll talk to Charlie."

"Choe, you're a champ," Delilah said as she gave him a quick hug.

< 64 >

17

MARK VISITS THE SEARCHERS AND CASSANDRA

June 18, 2018/10:00 a.m.

"Here's the situation, Mark," Carlos said. "We've found three more potential launch sites and probably more to come. Darlene, whom you have just met, is the hotshot cartographer behind all this. Your agency needs to understand the possible scope of future operations."

"The Mount Hyesan operation looks too dangerous to us right now, the way we've planned it," Choe added.

"We need a long-term approach and we need to have you meet and bond with this guy, 'Black Hand,'" Carlos said. "We are even thinking of the four of us going together to climb at Paekdusan or the Marble Mountains on a strictly tourist basis to take photos. Maybe we will create a dummy organization, and name it the North Korean Mountain Lovers or something like that, with a goal of publishing the book of photos later."

Carlos continued, "You need to learn some basic Korean and Chinese. We will help you with that as well as how to interact with these people. Black Hand is a grown-up kid. You will have to show him your drone and teach him how to fly it, and maybe you should carry an identical backup with your camera in it. Anyway, you have to loosen up and give yourself deep cover for the long haul."

"I like your ideas, guys," Mark replied. "My immediate boss is a believer in deep cover, but there's a lot of higher-ups that don't know what we're talking about."

"Tell your boss it's now or never," Carlos said. "We have to do the joint training gig right away because come July the summer monsoon season starts in Korea and it will be raining like crazy. Once you're trained you'll be better able to handle the monsoon and it will give you extra cover. Better brush up on your card games or dice until we find out what kind of rainy-day entertainment Black Hand is in to. I'm

< 65 >

sure he would love to visit a whorehouse but I doubt there are any out there in the wilds of North Korea."

Sometimes life gives you a break, and sometimes it breaks your heart. Mark felt sure life had given him his first big break when his bosses handed him a carte blanche on the goofy Searchers/Cassandra operation. A little chat between Mike Pompeo and Gina Haspel was responsible for that, but Mark didn't know that.

June 23, 2018
Mt. Kumgang Mountain Resort, North Korea

Carlos, Choe, Mark and Black Hand arrived at Mt. Kumgang on a special bus they picked up at the South Korean border. For three days they climbed and hiked, strictly adhering to all the restrictions regarding access. The weather was beautiful and so was the hiking. Mike took lots of pictures. They socialized in the evening. Their mountain club was noticed by others. Black Hand was in toy heaven as he learned to fly Mark's little drone airplane. He even painted a face on it resembling an angry mountain spirit.

June 27, 2018
Pyongyang Airport, North Korea

For the next four days they duplicated their Kumgang foray at Paekdusan. There were more people and trails there. As they left on July first, it looked and felt like the monsoon was coming. They were leaving just in time. Mark and Black Hand had become buddies and Choe and Carlos were pleased with their trainee. Black Hand was particularly pleased that Mark had introduced him to various new card games including that diabolical poker.

< 66 >

18

The President's Visit

August 28, 2018
Cassandra/Searchers Joint Meeting

The president dropped by to visit after hearing the new CIA director sing the praises of the unexpected and unconventional success of the Searchers' initiative.

"It turns out the North Koreans have way more hidden military sites than we expected," General Callahan informed the president. "We are, however, not surprised to find they are still building new missile installations in plain sight in Pyongyang."

"Using our protocol, Mr. President, we expect to find lots more sites in the coming months," Delilah Cummings added.

"I'm pleased with your success," replied the president. "I just wish we knew how strong these North Koreans are and how good their weapons."

"Why don't you ask them directly, sir," Carlos said. "Maybe show some skepticism of their claims and get them to brag about what they have. Or tell them only the strong can be transparent because they have nothing to hide. They might slip up and tell us more than they should."

"Interesting idea," Mike Pompeo said.

"The president is also interested in any ideas you might have to help him get the border wall built quickly. It's going too slow," John Bolton added.

"Sure," Charlie replied. "Build it cheaper. Don't assume every party of migrants is supplied with a bulldozer. Build high and strong only in very special crossing areas. Skinny walls but lots of border agents for patrols. Maybe you can hire some of the homeless to be auxiliary 'border watchers.'"

"Remember, Senator Heller from Nevada suggested you talk to

< 67 >

border patrol agents for ways to strengthen the wall and the border," Carlos added.

Darlene chimed in to the conversation, "And those interdiction towers or whatever they're called, little fire watch towers with electronic sensors, have been effective in some places."

John Bolton changed course, "On another subject, can you give us suggestions on how to solve our Iran problem? Secretary Mattis said you guys have some ideas on this subject."

"Sure do, sir, but you probably won't like our ideas," Carlos replied. "We don't believe there is an Iran problem. It's a mistaken notion we've inherited from prior administrations. Iran is no threat to us, and we really have no particular interest there. Revenge for past humiliation is hardly a worthy reason, and their threats are likely just bombast due to their personalities."

Carlos continued speaking, "Some people are afraid for some of our allies in that part of the world, like Israel, Saudi Arabia, and Turkey, that are opposed to Iran. But that should be of no concern to us. Israel could demolish the entire country of Iran in one hour any time they choose. Inshallah! They would have no qualms about using their nuclear arsenal, and they don't need help from us. Besides, they've embarrassed us by being unwilling to negotiate with the Palestinians, while we have been touting their good faith to the world.

"We should not have allies in the Middle East or elsewhere and should divest ourselves of those we do have. Friends are okay but allies mean treaties and treaties are like webs binding us to go to war for others. The Middle East is a historic trap for all kinds of unresolved ethnic, and religious, and political problems dating back centuries. It's like the Tar Baby in the Uncle Remus stories: the harder you punch it, the deeper you get enmeshed in the tar. We have wandered too far away from George Washington's advice against foreign entanglements."

Choe, Charlie, Delilah, and General Callahan nodded vigorously to show their agreement.

John Bolton did not like what he just heard and his face showed his displeasure, but with remarkable diplomatic aplomb, he replied, "Your views will take some serious thought."

Mike Pompeo interjected, "What about the Russian problem. Is the president headed in the right direction even though it might cost him votes or maybe the next election?"

"Yes," Charlie replied, as all nodded in agreement.

< 68 >

"The Cold War ended in nineteen ninety, but both of your parties, in recent years, have slowly restored the Cold War with the Russians," Choe said. "This was accomplished with the able assistance of the media. Why? Because you dispute Russia's actions in the Crimea, East Ukraine, and Syria, and that's in their sphere of influence, not yours. Your European friends have been fighting each other for hundreds and thousands of years over petty border disputes. Why should you join that fight?"

Choe continued his explanation. "Why do you return to the Cold War? Because some foolish young Russian men, trolls, computer hackers with an attitude, tried to trick and influence Americans into thinking better of their country. Do you think democracy is so fragile or are Americans too stupid to smell a con?"

Carlos interrupted. "No foreign power's second-rate propaganda unit can sow discord among us better than we can do to ourselves. As Pogo Possum used to say, "We have met the enemy and he is us!"

"It's irresponsible to put the world, and civilization, at risk over such petty disagreements," Choe said. "Nuclear war between America and Russia would destroy human civilization. However, one of your political parties has seen the opportunity to use this issue to defeat you politically. In doing that they have tapped into or channeled into the old Cold War hate and fear. Shame on them!"

"Mr. President," Carlos said, "I feel sure that future historians will approve your stance on the Russia question and give you a positive and secure place in the history books, but for the present I predict a continuing shit storm."

The president stood up slowly and the triumvirate exited. As they reached the door, Mike Pompeo said, "Thank you ladies and gentlemen for your comments."

After the presidential party had left the room, Choe said in a loud voice, "Let's hear it for Darlene, the human ferret, who made this day possible."

Choe's statement was followed by clapping and cheers. They all knew that Darlene wasn't embarrassed by the nickname, in fact, she loved it. Darlene had a knack for sniffing out these hidden military installations and thought it was more fun than a barrel of monkeys. She was living her own "Vida Loca." Everyone has to find their own.

< 69 >

19

FAMILY DOINGS IN SANTA FE

August 31, 2018
The Ordoñez Rancheria near Santa Fe, New Mexico

Carlos' father, Gilberto Ordoñez, had called him to come home if he was able because his mother had little time left and this could likely be his last opportunity to see her. This was not a surprise to Carlos since his mother was in the advanced stages of Alzheimer's. His father had been caring for her for the last eight years entirely on his own, except for the last year when he had hired a local PN to assist him for two to three hours per day.

Carlos and Sally took the first flight they could snag to Santa Fe where Mr. Ordoñez met them at the airport in his jeep. As they drove up the last curve and topped the ridge where the house stood, Sally could not restrain herself.

"Carlos, how can you stand to live in DC when you have this beautiful hacienda to come home to?"

"Well Sally, it's the other way around. I know if the Swamp spits me out I have this to come home to, and that gives me the patience to endure the Swamp a little longer."

"I understand, Carlitos. Señor Ordoñez, you have a lovely hacienda here."

"Gracias, dear lady," Mr. Ordoñez replied. And to get further plaudits from you, I will show you the rest of the casa and the gardens and the stable while Carlos goes to spend some time with his mama before we all sit down to a late dinner, Spanish style."

Dinner was simple but elegant. Teresa, Carlos' mom sat mute to his left at the table. She wore lovely clothes and jewelry partially covered by a large bib. Her stare was mostly vacant but occasionally there were glimmers of intelligence. Occasionally, she looked towards Sally on her right and smiled. Suddenly she spoke, "Linda! Linda!"

Sally looked at Carlos.

< 70 >

"She is saying you are beautiful," Carlos said.

"Gracias Teresa," Sally said to her as she gripped Teresa's hand.

Teresa unexpectedly responded, "Her soul is pure. She will make you happy but she has no children."

"No Teresa, I am not with child," Sally replied.

"You will face a great danger," Teresa continued.

Suddenly Teresa's face slumped forward into the soup bowl. Martha, the PN, was walking by and stopped. She lifted Teresa's head up, washed her face, and pulled the soup away. She and Gilberto lowered Teresa into the wheelchair and whisked her away to her bedroom.

Early the next morning as the exhausted and jetlagged Carlos and Sally finally awoke in Carlos' room, they heard an unusual amount of early morning bustle. As soon as they emerged from the room they knew something had happened. Teresa had died during the night and Gilberto was busy chatting with the village priest and the undertaker.

"You understand," Gilberto said to Carlos and Sally, "Teresa was a Catholic so I am honoring her wishes. For me, I wish to be cremated and buried in my own tierra. You know Teresa refused hospital and hospice. She would get hysterical any time I tried to take her away from her house, even for a checkup. I strongly suggest you two go back to DC now, on the next available plane. I'll get you to the airport. The logistics of dying are not something you need to get acquainted with at your age. You are welcome at any other time at a happier moment."

Señor Ordoñez, I want to tell you how highly I think of you for caring for Teresa as you have. Few men could have done it. I see now why Carlos is the man he is."

"I hope you're wrong, Sally. Doesn't the marriage promise say, 'for better or for worse, in sickness and in health, til death do us part?' Although I believe Henry the VIII did the world a service by making divorce possible for everybody especially since humans always make this kind of awful, primal mistake of choosing the wrong partner. I believe if you've made a good choice you should stick with it."

For this speech Sally thought Gilberto deserved two hugs. One right then and another when they parted at the airport.

On the plane back to DC Sally proposed an offer of marriage to Carlos. Carlos proved he had been thinking in the same direction when he pulled a gorgeous engagement ring out of his pocket like a stage magician. Gilberto, as magician's assistant, had provided Carlos

< 71 >

with his mother's engagement ring and other lovely baubles. Gilberto was a fast thinker and a long thinker.

"You're quicker to speak what's in your heart, my love," Carlos said. "I was afraid you might say no, so I hesitated."

Neither of them was ready to set an exact date but a Christmas wedding was tentatively scheduled by mutual consent.

< 72 >

20

MIDTERM FEVER

September 2018
Seoul, South Korea, Events—Real and Apocryphal

President Moon and Supreme Leader On met this month to discuss economic development loans for North Korea after North Korea's private talks with Japanese Investors collapsed. Requests by the North Korean women used as "comfort women" for Japanese soldiers were also turned down. The Japanese indicated the worsening world economic downturn was a major factor.

The United States government reminded the South Korean government that aid to South Korea could not be "passed through" to North Korea under any circumstances.

President Moon's modest package of proposed economic loans to North Korea met stiff political resistance but was passed.

Reconciliation fever was running high. Political theater was being performed. Ninety-year old South Koreans crossed into North Korea to be reunited with North Korean relatives. Kim theatrically criticized—like a critic of political corruption—his own leaders who could not get dams built on time to feed the people because water was in use elsewhere to feed the nuclear turbines.

The first vague timetable for North Korea's denuclearization was issued this month by Kim Jong Un. They are to denuclearize "by the end of Trump's first term." Was there a hidden message here? Was he saying he was confident now that Trump would win a second term? Was he buttering up the big T? Or was he in Chinese fashion being vague to obfuscate and pretend compliance? If Trump were to obtain a second term they would invariably claim that they would denuclearize by the end of his second term.

Also, this month Kim revived so-called 'mass games' for the celebration of North Korea's seventieth anniversary.

On September 9, when news of this new and clever PR

<73>

development became widely publicized, Carlos, Choe and Charlie had a brief chat about it. Choe had seen a small piece of one of these performance's years ago.

"Looked like a cross between Tai Chi and a Shinto shrine harvest festival," Choe said. "Very strange, like watching *Mondo Cane*."

Carlos said, "Some have criticized the 'games' as a homage to authoritarianism. I agree with that characterization but I wouldn't call them games at all. No one is having fun; they are a religious mass dance pantomime, a throwback mélange of Shintoism and Buddhism. An unthinking insectile group grok."

They speculated about what in history it could be compared to. The goose-step flag waving, boot stomping and speechifying at the Reichstag? The incidence of tarantism in Southern Italy in the 16th and 17th centuries, with its unexplainable dancing and mass hysteria?

Charlie proposed a prosaic reason for the "success of the games." "Perhaps participants received an extra ration of food. Maybe people were dancing for their supper," Charlie said.

On September 30, Mr. Ri, diplomat for North Korea at the U.N. General Assembly said the North does not see a 'corresponding response' from the U.S. to North Korea's early disarmament moves.

Carlos' response was, "What moonshine! There have been no disarmament moves."

Charlie laughed. "Do you think he means when they blew up that testing tower they didn't need any longer, as a publicity stunt?"

"You know," Carlos said, "Trump's maybe the right kind of shoe—thumping Krushchev diplomat we need to deal with slippery Kim. Or, he might just keep Kim on a leash and leave the hard issues for later presidents, making historians weep for lost opportunity. Only time will tell."

October 15, 2018
The White House, Washington, DC

The president crowed about his hard-won victory in getting Kavanaugh finally approved as Supreme Court Justice. He also predicted the Dems delaying tactics would hurt them at midterms.

< 74 >

October 23, 2018
The White House, Washington, DC

The U.S. president chided North Korea today for failing to negotiate in good faith. All discussions and meetings since June 12 had resulted in no progress whatsoever and only the vaguest of timetables. The president, despite receiving 'pretty letters' from Kim, challenged the North Korean government to openly disclose the location of all its nuclear, ICBM, and short/medium/long-range missile launch sites, and identify the targets of each. The president said unless people knew this they could not even begin to trust the North Koreans.

The Democratic party and the media poo-pooed the president's action and called it sophomoric and an attempt to hijack the midterms, but the public loved it.

November 6, 2018
Midterm Elections

Democrats took the House and the Republicans kept the Senate. An unfortunate recipe for legislative gridlock. Impeachment fever waned, replaced by a new hope of impending victory in 2020, and forgetting the queer duck in the White House was not lame. All Doctor Doolittle Mueller, the famed ornithologist could say was, "Quack! Quack! He's a Muscovy duck!"

Comic books fans know better. The Donald is a reincarnation of Howard the Duck.

November 10, 2018
Washington, DC, Sally's Apartment, 6:00 p.m.

The moment Carlos walked in he knew something was wrong. He noticed that Sally had been crying so he gave her a hug.

"What's wrong, Sally? Digame."

Sally tried to dry her eyes but the tears kept pouring out. Carlos let her cry until the emotion was spent.

"You remember Carlos, what your mother said that night?"

"Of course."

"She said, 'But she has no children.' That reminded me of something I knew about my extensive family genealogy, that some

< 75 >

branches of it ended up childless. I went to a reproductive specialist and she confirmed I am one of them. I am totally sterile and can't have any children."

She finished speaking and the tears flowed anew. With a flourish she pulled off her engagement ring and give it back to a stunned Carlos.

"Here Carlos, take this back. Give it to some woman who can bear you children. Like Delilah. She wants to have a boy and a girl. And you know of course, she's in love with you."

"I was afraid of that, but love is not an incurable disease you know. She also has a tendre for Charlie but she does not think he's strong enough for her. She doesn't know him as well as I do. He blushes easily and appears to be easily flustered, but beneath that veneer of affability he is rock solid on issues that matter."

Carlos hugged her again and gently placed the ring back on her finger. "Sweet Sally, listen to me. You bewitched me in the first three minutes of our relationship and nothing or no one has changed that. I have no particular desire to be a parent or have my name live on, or any of those old values that purportedly meant so much to men in prior times. It's sort of my fault for this little crisis scene because I did not talk about this stuff with you sooner. I didn't want to rush our relationship. We can do plenty for the world by pursuing our separate careers and not adding another person to the roster of our overcrowded planet. Think about it and let me know. I think we need to set a date. How about getting married next month on Christmas Eve? How and where I leave up to you."

Sally hugged him fiercely. "Yes to both. The how and where part we'll both think about."

"We'll make our first announcement to the gang at the Red Dragon," Carlos said. "And it's about time you show them that flasher on your finger."

Since they had not announced their engagement Sally had not been wearing the ring, except at work where she used it to deflect the tiresome advances of unattached male staff members. The size and weight of the ring was a message and had given Sally more peace than she had ever enjoyed.

Her other problem was with her patients. Numerous male patients and a couple female had become infatuated with her and had to be shifted to one of her colleagues, Laurel or Hardy (depending on

< 76 >

the patient's sex, age, and nature of infatuation). Dr. Laurel Smythe was brilliant, warm, but sexless and plain as a potato. Dr. Abraham Hardy looked like an ex-boxer or mafia enforcer and would have been a runner-up in any neighborhood 'Mr. Ugly' contest. The beautiful people did not send their children or themselves to these two very talented shrinks until later, after the flashy folk had fumbled the ball.

< 77 >

21

CASSANDRA DOES DOMESTIC

April 1, 2019
The Pentagon

When General Callahan got a telephone call from Mike Pompeo giving Cassandra new directions to investigate, he at first thought Mike was pulling his leg. After all, it was April Fool's Day.

"Did I hear you right sir, you want us to look into Obamacare?"

"Yes, General. You see, this issue is dividing our party and upping the morale of the democrats. The usual political give and take is not working on this one. You guys look at things differently than most people. Maybe you can think of something to make everybody happy."

"We will give it a try, sir. Anything else?"

"See," Mike said, "if you can think of any infrastructure projects at 100% federal reimbursement that would be popular. We would appreciate it. Everyone is pitching their own partisan stuff these days and we can't get wide agreement on anything. Also, can you give me pointers to refute these 'holier than thou' sanctuary state people?"

Mike continued before he got an answer. "We're looking for some policy issue or program we can get behind that's positive and helps people. We won't be able to meet with you for a month so my secretary will get back to you tomorrow to give you the date. So... whoops! I almost forgot. John just suggested you guys look into the possibility that South Korea might voluntarily reunite with North Korea. Although farfetched, it could give us kittens if it happened."

"Yes sir, we'll start looking into these issues right away. I have a meeting with my Cassandra Group in fifteen minutes."

At first, General Callahan got a lot of laughter out of his staff about their new assignments. After a while they settled down and realized they had some worthwhile new opportunities. General Callahan knew his group always had their 'thinking caps' on and had given thought to many issues before being presented with them in

<78>

conference. This assignment was different. Original thinking was harder to conjure but he had great faith in his team.

After the meeting, Choe patted Carlos on the back and kidded him. "How's the old married man doing?"

Carlos patted him on the back in return and grinned. "I may be married but I'm not old, you young squirt. I think we both are off-weight and in need of physical conditioning, old hoss."

"Maybe you're right Kimosabe," Choe replied. "Charlie and I are going to escort Delilah and Darlene on a visit to Seoul in two weeks. We are going to confer with Francie and Red Hand on a bunch of stuff that just can't get done long distance."

"Maybe this is a good time for you and me to get in some serious sparring," Carlos said. "Why don't we start tonight and drop the Red Dragon for the next two Saturdays. Maybe we should do a self-defense training for Charlie, Delilah, Darlene and Sally. For some reason, I'm nervous about your upcoming trip. One of your Korean newspapers has compared Seoul to Chicago, decrying the sour fruits of affluence."

"Let's do it," Choe replied. "They could probably use a 'Touch of Zen. You are a worry wart Carlos, but you could be right."

Precognition, second sight, whenever you call it, Carlos apparently had it. Choe's group was set upon in Seoul by a nasty mob of tipsy or drug-crazed youth. Delilah was nearly abducted but Charlie made such good use of his newfound martial arts skills that he finally floored all of her would-be abductors. He protected Delilah with his body as he and Choe knocked out the remaining youngsters who were trying to abduct her. Choe said they looked like upper-middle class kids and he even recognized one. Meanwhile, according to Choe, Darlene single-handedly took on one male and two females. She cold-cocked the male with a smashing right-left to the jaw and body slammed and pinned both astounded young women.

Most young job seekers are guilty of 'inflative poofery' on their resumes. Darlene went the other way. She had neglected to mention in a resume that she had grown up on a real farm and had been the top wrestler on her high school team. Her brother was a Golden Gloves champ. Should she ever leave the Searchers she had a guaranteed career in mixed martial arts.

As they drove away from this awful encounter before the police could arrive, Delilah hugged Charlie and Darlene to her with all her might and cried shamelessly.

< 79 >

No one was surprised three months later to hear that Delilah and Charlie were engaged.

April 29, 2019/11:00 a.m.
Cassandra Meets the Triumvirate

General Callahan was a little worried; he had gone to the meeting room early to think. His trio of generalist world historians had not come up with much that the big bosses would like regarding Obamacare and their other assignments except the reunification one. His staff considered Obamacare to be a political 'tar baby' issue. How can you dump a people program that's up and running (or limping along) which helps some of the people some of the time but at huge expense? Very carefully? Could you throw out the bathwater without dumping the baby?

Ultimately, General Callahan did not care whether he was jobless this afternoon. He had his own personal principles that guided his behavior. One of these was: he would do the job right and the way he saw fit. The world was full of "yes" men and now "yes" women, and toadies of all sexes.

He thought his staff's ideas were ingenious but would require considerable political risk-taking. Sugar coating the truth could give you diabetes of the brain. General Callahan had many notions that would have branded him that awful appellation of "liberal" (whatever that means today). He believed oil drilling in the Arctic Ocean was foolhardy and in the Arctic Wildlife Refuge, a damn shame.

He believed women had a right to abortion and birth control and weren't about to give that up. The silly crusade against Planned Parenthood would ultimately prove counterproductive to a bedroom-peeking government. He also supported the Pope's injunction that we should clean up the oceans that humans had crapped up.

Callahan never let his opinions on any subject be known at work or interfere with his objectivity (like public servants used to be).

The president's party arrived twenty minutes late, and after a perfunctory introduction, started right in with an unexpected curveball for General Callahan from John Bolton.

"General Callahan," said Mr. Bolton, "we have been fighting with our intel chiefs over Afghanistan. As a former military commander, what is your opinion of our present mission in that country? Should we stay or leave?"

< 80 >

General Callahan smiled. "It's a waste of time, money and our soldiers' lives. We should've gotten out long ago. The Middle East and particularly Syria and Afghanistan are 'tar babies.' We should pull out of Afghanistan and let the current government work things out with the Taliban. Look at the historical record. Afghanistan was a 'tar baby' to the Russians too."

The smile on John Bolton's face told him he had scored big points. That would help with the bitter medicine shortly to be dispensed.

"Thank you, General. Your opinion is much appreciated."

General Callahan nodded to Charlie who started the ball rolling.

"Mr. President," Charlie said, "we all think there is no way to 'fix' Obamacare. It's already such a colossal Rube Goldberg contraption. Further tinkering with it even by a magician or a grand jury is not likely to achieve anything of lasting worth. Obamacare should be dumped in the ashcan of history as a daring failure. Although it helped some people it did not mainly benefit individual citizens but large corporate entities that make money out of medical care. What it provided was not medical care for people but medical insurance eligibility, usually with high co-pays and deductibles. The presence of these made its official title 'The Affordable Care Act' a total misnomer."

"If you still can't get people to face this failure," Choe said, "you need to suggest the collection of new data from the program such as how many persons were on an Obamacare-obtained medical plan and did not in the entire eligibility year receive any cash benefit or service from their plan. Some couples could go an entire year paying six hundred dollars monthly for premiums and because of the plan's five thousand dollar yearly deductible, got nothing from it. The other data point could be how many people got more from their plan moneywise than they put into it in premiums, copays and deductibles. I doubt this number is very high."

Carlos entered the conversation, "Ask yourself this, who are the Obamacare winners? Here's one: the extreme case of Myrtle. She buys a plan that costs a thousand dollars per month and has no deductible so when they find she has terminal brain cancer after fifty thousand dollars worth of diagnostic expenses she is clearly a winner because her treatment should she choose to have it will cost a few hundred thousand dollars more. She's even further ahead and has plenty of time to plan her funeral, but no money to pay for it."

Carlos continues. "The data set you want to collect is not that

< 81 >

of the winners, but the non-winners. That's the percentage of people on Obamacare who got no reimbursement or a trifling amount that is less than the premiums they paid. Oh sure, they were covered by insurance and that stands for something, at least in the world of CPAs and actuaries. But in the real world when someone gets real sick with diabetes or heart attack they will get a nine-one-one ride to the nearest available hospital regardless of their insurance coverage. While admitting them to the hospital saved their life it causes the person to end up in bankruptcy and leaves the hospital with costs they have to eat."

"With a view to these kinds of numbers," Charlie says, "the pertinent question is: should the government subsidize medical insurance at all or should it subsidize medical care for real people. But the cleverness of the democrats that crafted the hodgepodge that is Obamacare cannot be ignored. Linking new federal support money for Medicaid with Obamacare 'basic' was brilliant because care for sick, poor people is a winner. Support for medical insurance for modestly poor people is not a sure thing. The big winners are the medical insurance corporations. The bottom line is Obamacare is too expensive. It develops too little bang for the government's deficit-financed buck. Most of the voters on both sides of the aisle know that thirty-two trillion dollars to finance Medicare for all is more of the same. What's needed is a stop-gap medical plan, one that interfaces with the current medical system but does not compete with it."

"Here's that three-point plan," explained General Callahan. "First, end Obamacare; second, grow the Medicaid program again; and third, develop a national health service targeted to splinter populations. Keep any pieces of Obamacare you can tolerate such as the 'pre-existing condition' rule which seems popular with voters. Offer states up to a hundred percents federal funding for quality and cost-effectiveness of Medicaid programs. A professor at the University of Chicago's School of Social Service Administration has already suggested this avenue, so you would have some support already from the democratic left before you even start. Theoretically. Develop a limited scope national health service, funded and run by the federal government to provide direct medical services to splinter populations not reached by the country's other systems. This program would be totally office-based care, no hospital care at all. Only requirements are U.S. citizenship and unmet medical need. These walk-in urgent care

< 82 >

clinics would divert people who would have gone to regular hospital emergency rooms without insurance. Clinics would offer two kinds of admissions, 'swab and clean' minor injuries and life-threatening admissions of very ill or comatose individuals at risk of dying. Most of the 'deadly admissions' are due to people not aware they have diabetes, high blood pressure, or a heart condition, etc. and are not medicated for these. The urgent care function of these clinics would save hospital-based medical corporations considerable money. This means the national health service would complement and assist these entities and certainly not compete with them. Office-based care would focus on keeping the chronically ill medicated and able to function without hospitalization."

Carlos spoke next. "The centerpiece of this national health service would be the opening of 'respite centers' to service the homeless, particularly the homeless who are mentally ill, using a simplified model of a settlement house, as these were used in Chicago and New York in the 19th century. Previous promises to fund clinics for the mentally ill, outside of hospital settings, have proven to be useless where they ever existed at all. Kicking all these people out of mental hospitals has resulted in their receiving 'iron boot therapy' on the streets and in prisons instead of the medication and gentle medical supervision they need to stay sane. On the streets they suffer the humiliation of walking in human feces and other garbage. They face daily fear of losing all their possessions and what sanity they might have left. And for the majority of homeless who are not mentally ill, they are living in a psychological hell which comes from tent city concentration camps where society's usual guarantee of personal safety seldom holds.

What would be needed here? Bathrooms and trashcans, and more bathrooms. Supervision and counseling for those who seek it. A chance to read magazines or books or watch television or use the internet. A kitchen or food dispensary. A laundry. A security staff sufficient to ensure rights of staff and customers. Mental health professionals and social workers to help those who want to exit their situation. Facility workers who could be hired from the ranks of the homeless."

"What is not wanted?" asked Charlie. "Real estate and buildings. Use mobile homes, trailers and porta-potties to keep costs down. Use eminent domain on a temporary basis at the inner-city locations. Insist on adherence to public health laws."

< 83 >

"Another goal," offered Carlos, "is to move homeless people, who are willing, out of the central city and into government supervised 'hobo camps' on federal land adjacent to the city. The much-despised BLM had done this Samaritan kind of thing quietly for many years. In parts of the west, 'camper homeless' people congregate and squat free on BLM land, mostly desert, and have done so for years. Most are without transportation, are disabled or elderly, and permanently homeless. Their temporary homes are camper shells, sheds, tents, lean-tos, and busted vehicles. A patch of scrub they can call 'home' also gives them some dignity."

Carlos continued, "Mr. President, in our cursory look at the issue we noted that some years ago California had the foresight to raise tons of money for mental health but inexplicably they haven't spent it. It's clear the mentally ill are a sizable component of the homeless population in California which has given parts of Los Angeles and other major cities the 'fragrance' of Fresno. It would be nice to see Uncle Sam lead California to do right on this issue."

"As for what infrastructure program to back," said Choe, "you can build all respite centers, or all bathrooms, or a combination of the two. Both programs are positive and help people. Both will contribute permanent assets to your citizens as well as ameliorating current problems."

"That concludes our formal presentation," General Callahan said. "Any questions or comments?" He figured within sixty seconds he would know whether he still had a job.

There was a profound silence in the room for a whole minute. Then longer. This is much too long, General Callahan thought to himself, unless they are positively stunned speechless by our presentation.

John Bolton was the first to recover. "You guys are a little crazy sometimes but I'll be damned if I don't think you've got something there. Have to think about it."

Mike Pompeo spoke up next. "Could we really do something like this?"

Carlos deftly commented, "The democrats have people believing they want medical insurance but I'll bet they would prefer medical care instead."

"Carlos," General Callahan said, "can you deal with the question regarding the 'holier than thou' people who support the sanctuary state?"

< 84 >

Carlos nodded. "People who support sanctuary want to believe their cause is holy. Not so. Sanctuary states are the new confederacy. In the old days their soldiers wore grey. Now they are blue states, wearing the color belonging to the federal soldiers. Like the old confederate states of the union, they believe the federal government has no right to control the national borders or make laws to govern the whole. The old confederacy protected slave owners; the current one, centered in old California, protects criminals and trespassers, and encourages its citizens to tear down the war monuments and statues of the old confederacy. Their forefathers bled for their cause. Adding pharisaical hypocrisy to political myopia. Only barbarians destroy the cultural monuments of others."

"Enough with the domestic headaches," said General Callahan. "You wanted us to discuss whether we see a possibility that South Korea will voluntarily reunite with North Korea."

"Yes. It's unlikely but possible," Choe said. "Kim is actively pursuing his reunification card all the time. President Moon Jae In would love to be recognized as the leader who reunited his people but it would be like a goat lying down for a nap with a tiger."

"The power of psychological denial is very strong," Carlos said. "I could see this happening."

"Where would it leave us?" asked John Bolton.

"Up Schitz Creek without a paddle, sir," Carlos replied.

"He's right," Charlie said. "If the Koreas politically reunite Uncle Sam can no longer shelter South Korea with his nuclear umbrella nor do anything to protect it. National sovereignty. We would have to exit this part of Asia."

"There is a way we could exit and leave that part of the world more stabilized," Carlos said. We could give South Korea and Japan five nuclear missiles apiece to protect themselves. Our parting present to them. Take them out of the batch of nukes we are destroying under SALT. This will reduce ours and Russia's excess nukes. We probably should have done this years ago, or when we found out our unintelligent intel chiefs were wrong when they thought North Korea couldn't even build a tinker toy."

The president chuckled quietly to himself at Carlos' comment before his entourage quietly exited.

When General Callahan thought they were gone, he asked Carlos, "Ola lobo, donde estan?"

< 85 >

"Muy lejos amigo, they're out of earshot."

"Then we're lucky we didn't get fired today. You guys did brilliantly. If we're all still employed by next Saturday I'll cover your tabs at the Red Dragon. Carlos, your final comment was perfectly timed. You have a knack for diplomacy.

"General," Choe said, "he's a chip off the old family block. Did I get that slang right Carlitos?"

"Si mi amigo," replied Carlos.

< 86 >

22

Trouble in Seoul

August 15, 2020
The Triumvirate Meets with Cassandra

The president, John Bolton, and Mike Pompeo had last met with the Cassandra Group a long time ago on April 29, 2019. The president requested this Ides of August meeting because conditions in South Korea were deteriorating and his reelection campaign was in periodic crisis. He wanted the opinions of people he could trust to be objective and not just feedback of what he wanted to hear.

After the introductions, the president started right in. "What I'm hearing about South Korea makes me nervous. Are those guys going crazy over there? What's your take on that political situation? Are we in trouble over there?"

No one was eager to speak first.

General Callahan finally spoke, "Carlos, jump in. Remember that computer conversation we had first thing this morning with Francie."

"Our associate in Seoul," Carlos explained, "was saying that internal politics were highly scrambled in South Korea these days and getting worse. As she sees it, a majority of South Koreans are fed up with President Moon and his policies of reconciliation with North Korea at any cost. North Korea has promised much but has refused to sit down and negotiate seriously with the U.S. Therefore, no one wants to hand out further development money funds or any funds. And North Korea's harvest for this summer is looking poor."

"Mr. President," Charlie said, "your reelection campaign is a major topic in South Korean politics. President Moon has listened to U.S. House and Senate Democrats who say they are going to swamp you and defeat you in November and toss you out of the swamp. Moon thinks that getting rid of you will result in a quick, easy, bloodless reconciliation with North Korea."

"But that's absurd," said Mike Pompeo. "Isn't it, General Callahan?"

< 87 >

"Yes sir, the historical record seems to indicate that."

"A key question then," said the president, "is whether I am going to be re-elected. What are your candid thoughts on that subject?"

"That's easy sir," General Callahan replied. "We discussed that this morning before you came. All of us believe you will be re-elected but it will be close. Many democrats wish Jimmy Carter was twenty-five years younger. He recently cautioned his party to not go so far left that they couldn't find their way home. Warren and Pelosi don't have the deplorable baggage your previous opponent did. Neither does Mr. Sanders, personally. However, the economic/political muddle in Venezuela has hurt him because it has re-demonized the word 'socialism.' He suffers guilt by association. Mr. Perez's time hasn't come. Al Gore and Jerry Brown maybe are thinking about running, and a Mr. Shultz and Mayor Bloomberg. And maybe even Hillary?"

"None of these people have any new ideas and they are not up to dealing with the problems of the porous border, world politics, the threat of North Korea, or the tinderbox in the Middle East. They have also forgotten, or never realized, that your first victory was possible only because many democrats crossed over to vote for you. Many of these people are still registered as democrats and willing to forego political party to vote again for the candidate of their choice. Meanwhile, the bulk of the democrats are thinking of you as they sing, 'I'm gonna wash that man right out of my hair.'"

"Mr. President," Choe said, "the importance of your winning is that it will crash President Moon's political career and put Kim Jong Un in a tight space as well. He depends on Moon and South Korean social and entertainment figures for much of his support. That should quickly evaporate with your win."

"It would be a good time for Kim to switch to a provocative act, even a limited act of war to restore his country's belief in him," Carlos said.

"You mean he might attack us?" asked John Bolton.

"Not an all-out attack, I wouldn't think," replied Charlie.

"Perhaps a few missiles hitting one of our ships or Guam's airport, or an attack on one of our submarines?" asked General Callahan.

Carlos, Choe and Charlie all nodded.

"Mr. President," Carlos said, "this might be the opportunity to slam Kim with Sanction D without starting World War III, if you're lucky. You better act fast before Russia and China figure out what's happening."

< 88 >

"Remember sir," John Bolton said to the president, "I called Sanction D the 'Devil's Own.'"

"Tell me more, Carlos," the president said.

"First, you have to publicly warn North Korea that any attacks against the United States no matter how small, may result in 'total' response. The reason for this is Kim might attack a low-profile U.S. target in order to bolster his flagging image with his people, but without, he hopes, eliciting a major or a total response from the U.S. He can't be allowed to do that. If he strikes a South Korean or even Japanese target we should help those countries strike back with greater force without directly involving U.S. servicemen."

"Second," Carlos continued, "you establish a separate entity within our military command that constantly monitors North Korean missile launches or military activity and immediately certifies them by issuing automatic press releases timed and dated to the second."

"Third," Carlos said, "you issue advance orders that require an immediate military response be made under certain simple conditions such as a missile headed towards anything of ours without consulting with headquarters for authorization to attack. This part, because it goes against custom, will be the hardest to achieve, but this is the key to real victory."

"If we act quickly, the war could be over in one hour," said General Callahan. "The faster our response, the fewer nuclear casualties the U.S. will sustain. The secret is hitting them before most of their missiles are launched and having broadcast the incontrovertible proof that they started it but we acted faster to finish it. Your decision in October of twenty eighteen, which was reported by Secretary Mattis to deploy mid-range nuclear cruise missiles to Navy ships will be a game-changer when the war whistle blows."

"General Callahan, what do you think are the chances that North Korea will attack us in some way when the president is reelected?" Mike Pompeo asked.

General Callahan looked around the table and said, "Fifty-fifty." He was answered by three thumbs up.

"Gentlemen," Mike Pompeo said, "you've given us much to think about. Mr. President, did you want to continue the discussion or are we through for now?"

"You're right, Mike. It's time to go."

< 89 >

23

Beijing's Bane

September 13, 2020
Francie Hears About "Beijing's Bane"

Francie sent Delilah and General Callahan a credible report alleging a hidden launch site had a "cradle" for "Beijing's Bane." North Korean staff gossip had many workers upset by this discovery. Two of that site's workers had independently defected, lured jointly by distaste for the targeting and by the offer of gold. One of the defectors was half-Chinese, half-Korean, the other was Korean only. Both were questioned under rigid professional lie detector interrogation. Later, Francie questioned them with Red Hand for two more hours, separately and individually. Red Hand knew one of the workers by reputation as a "reliable person." Francie promised them a hundred gold coins each, the moment their stories could be verified.

The CIA was immediately alerted. General Callahan was dubious they would respond. To his surprise they did so immediately; he figured they must have had some information on their own. Mark Canfield and Black Hand were paired with Chang Low, a Chinese nuclear expert and spy, with eight backup agents. This plan involved breaking in to the purported 'bane' site if they could not bureaucratically try and talk their way in.

On September 20, they fought their way in and Chang Low confirmed the targeting was aimed at Beijing. Mark reported this immediately by satellite phone to CIA headquarters. While Chang phoned in his confirmation, Mark covered him, for his first taste of James Bond work. They fought their way out of the facility and only Mark, Chang and Black Hand made it. Mark was mortally wounded and did not survive the helicopter ride home. Chang and Black were hospitalized for weeks recovering from multiple bullet wounds.

Mark's funeral was held on the morning of September 30 in a Washington DC location and he was honored by his associates at the

< 90 >

nearby CIA headquarters as well as the entire Cassandra Group and the Searchers. Plans went forward for the posthumous publication of Mark's photo book entitled *The Mountains of North Korean*. The fool volunteering for this onerous task was Hanna, Mark's older sister, showing the depths of sisterly love. Choe and Carlos told her they would send her all their photos too. At which point she broke down and started crying again, to be enfolded by her family.

Carlos and Choe walked away with tears in their eyes. They too would miss Mark.

September 20, 2020
The Russians Strike Suddenly

The Russians had been notified on September 20 of the results of the "Bane" raid. They surprised everyone by conducting simultaneous mass commando raids on the afternoon of September 30 at ten launch locations which they had vaguely suspected for years. Of the ten sites, nine had missiles aimed at the U.S. and one aimed at Moscow. That was enough. Das vidana!

October 1, 2020
The Big 3 Meets in Moscow

Putin, Jinping, and the U.S. president met face to face in Moscow to discuss mutual security issues. It was secretly and unanimously decided that North Korea was a severe threat to the entire world and the three major nations would unite against that threat. The press was told only that this was a routine discussion of general issues, the first of others to come.

October 4, 2020
U.S. War Declaration Requested by the President

The U.S. president asked Congress to approve a Declaration of War against the rogue nation of North Korea, which the president labeled "an imminent threat to the security of the United States." The democrats immediately denounced this as an irresponsible act and an attempt to hijack the upcoming election. The implacable "I" word was used profusely...and rancorously.

< 91 >

24

ELECTION DAY AND BANANAS

November 3, 2020
Election Day

The U.S. president was voted in for his second term. This time he won both the Electoral College votes and the popular votes. The democratic party and the media were stunned once again disbelieving that lightning could strike twice, or traitors prosper. "War is the Unfolding of Miscalculation." (Barbara Tuchman, historian)

November 25, 2020/10:19 a.m.
Cassandra Meets Bananas on the Menu

The Cassandra Group had been meeting and arguing since eight in the morning. Charlie was uncertain the North Koreans were now ready to press the first strike button. It bothered his beliefs in rationality and the human survival instinct. Choe felt they were ready but Carlos vacillated which was unusual for him.

General Callahan turned to Carlos and said, "Amigo Numantia are they going to do it?"

"Carajo, como se yo?" His face slowly changed to a grimace and he suddenly said, "Yes General, they're going to do it. I've had a sudden feeling of bleak certainty in my gut. If this is what it's like to have a 'sixth sense' then it hurts bigtime. Afghanistan banana-stand."

When Charlie looked at Carlos' face, he suddenly knew Carlos was right.

All four members of the Cassandra Group were of the same opinion. It was time to pass on the Afghanistan banana-stand message to the president. Kim Jong Un was reportedly very depressed by the president's reelection victory. Even before that, many were of the opinion that he was like a householder who had painted himself into a corner with no way out. He even had difficulty selling his weaponry on

< 92 >

the black market. Buyers were unsure of its reliability and effectiveness, and North Korea was a touchy seller. It looked like a 'use it or lose it' situation. After all, what was war merchandise for—if not to make war?

"North Korea doesn't have a Q bomb but it looks like they are going to be "The Mouse that Roared." Choe said.

"This may turn out to be the most confusing war we ever fought," said Carlos. "No one knows if North Korea's nukes and ICBMs are reliable and effective and whether they can get all the way across the Pacific. Even they probably don't know. They had lots of problems in testing except where they copied reliable Russian models. We don't know how good their quality control is either, or how many reliable Russian rocket engines they were able to get to North Korea."

"All they need," said Charlie, "is for only a few to get through to do massive damage."

"Could even bankrupt the country," Choe said.

"Look on the bright side guys," Carlos said, "the Searchers have found thirty-three hidden sites of which twenty-six were ICBM sites. We've saved millions of American lives though our countrymen may never hear about us. We've been assured these sites would be hit first and hardest."

General Callahan got up abruptly. "Gentlemen continue the discussion. I'll go have my secretary send our message to the president first and come back for the rest of the discussion."

As General Callahan left the room, Charlie asked Carlos, "Do you think we're making history here or mischief?"

"Both. But you can't make an omelet without breaking some eggs. If this coming war turns out better than half-right for our president and our country, he will have his place in the history books. The words of CNN, Mueller, and millions of angry words of criticism won't matter. He will have destroyed the twentieth century's last awful world fascism."

"I agree," said Choe.

"I think you're both right," Charlie said. "Historians look for results, not political correctness."

< 93 >

25

CARLOS SNIFFS ARMAGEDDON

November 28, 2020
Carlos Sniffs the Wind

Carlos often checked out newspaper headlines in the early morning to get a feel for what was happening in the wider world. This morning's scan took longer than usual. By the time he reached the rest of the Cassandra Group he was visibly agitated, a total rarity for him.

"I'm afraid guys, this is going to be the day," he said.

"Really?" Choe asked. What makes you think so?"

"I don't know. Maybe what I read in the papers this morning but more likely something in my head. Or in my senses somehow. I'm picking up some kind of dangerous vibrations."

"I read those same headlines," Charlie said. "Seemed like the same old screwed up world."

"Let me go talk to Mario, the communications specialist. He's got to know to stay on his toes today," Carlos said.

"Go ahead amigo," General Callahan said. "Sally said your gift is real and I believe Sally."   Carlos had just finished talking to Mario, who was his usual snippy, sneering self. Carlos headed for a chair in the employee's lounge nearby. Carlos had a direct line of sight to Mario and Mario saw him as well, and grimaced to confirm it.

Suddenly a loud "pop" in Carlos' ear distracted his heavy thoughts. Someone was pouring a glass of champagne near his ear.

"Hi ya handsome." It was Sultry Sara the computer operator with a reputation as a man-killer and coup counter in the sexual wars.

The screaming voice of Mario interrupted this delicate encounter.

"Carlos, you son of a bitch, there's a flight of ICBMs heading eastward across the Pacific!"

Carlos took the offered glass, scarfed down the champagne all at once, handed it back and said, "Thanks! Gotta go now!"

He headed towards the screaming voice. Now we are really in for it, he thought. Sometimes it's no fun to be right.

< 94 >

November 28, 2020/7:37 p.m.
The War Room at the Pentagon

The large room was abuzz with noise, people were talking, yelling and joking. The large map on the wall was glowing with lines and symbols showing the results of today's military actions. There was a festive air like a victory party after a homecoming game. To an expert eye the board did look good if you didn't look at the civilian casualty list.

General Callahan raised his voice above the hubbub. "Ladies and gentlemen, the president and Secretary Mattis are in the room. All of you not on console duty please stand!"

Everyone stood up and a spontaneous round of applause broke out. Many voices cried out, "Hail to the Chief!" and the air was filled with cheers.

An older voice yelled, "Way to go, Mad Dog!"

The president, truly touched with this untypical and unexpected response, mixed with the people, shaking hands, much to the shock and horror of the Secret Service.

As the president's entourage approached, General Callahan saluted and shook hands with the president and Secretary Mattis.

"General Callahan, how does it look?" asked the president.

"Better than we could have expected, sir. From a strictly military point of view we beat the crap out of them. Could you and Secretary Mattis come with me to that conference room behind me where the Cassandra Group is waiting so we can give you a feel for the numbers before you talk to the press? And we need to take a peek into the near future as well."

General Callahan could see the relief on the faces of the Secret Service agents as the president waved goodbye to the crowd.

In the conference room, Carlos rattled off the pertinent facts and figures.

"As far as we know all North Korean launch installations are out of commission. Pyongyang was vaporized by a hydrogen bomb dropped by a B-1. North Korean military casualties are pegged at half a million, civilian casualties the same. Honolulu was destroyed and four of their nukes reached the continental U.S. in a random pattern. They were probably aimed at military targets but no military targets were

< 95 >

damaged, all damage was civilian. It's likely ten million Americans are dead but we probably won't have a reliable number for months. Compared to any war of the past this is a frighteningly high number. It is low compared to what it could have been. We estimate your 'automatic strike' order saved an additional sixty million American lives. Our missile shield stopped nothing. The important thing to remember besides the numbers is the U.S. is no longer susceptible to nuclear blackmail by North Korea. A loaded gun is no longer pointed at Uncle Sam's head, or anyone else's."

Choe spoke next. "In the future when all the facts and players are known, I believe history will award you the laurels you deserve even if the Nobel Committee is asleep. But, for the immediate future expect a political tsunami. You're going to have to order martial law and containment orders for the five hit zones and assist the states as they deal with saving the savable, counting the dead, and keeping radioactive traumatized citizens in quarantine while we try and help them recover. And in Korea, you need to make it known that any movement by the remaining North Korean army towards the DMZ will cause them to be nuked by your newly developed 'anti-personnel' nuke."

Charlie added, "You need to pow-wow with your buddies, Mr. Jinping and Mr. Putin, about the future of North Korea right away so that no one can accuse you of allowing genocide to occur by famine."

Mike, John and the president looked quite thoughtful after hearing Charlie's spiel.

< 96 >

26

Saving the North Korean People

November 29, 2020/11:00 a.m.
The Pentagon

General Callahan ordered everybody to sleep in this morning so their morning meeting started late. They were all better for their clan leader's foresight. People seldom understand how emotional stress slows down their ability to think clearly. Callahan had seen it in a war zone before.

"Let's start this morning with a brainstorming session on the future of North Korea," General Callahan said.

"We need to make sure all the old guard leaders are dead," said Choe. "Encourage people to take direct action. Vigilante time. We don't have the cultural background to do a 'Judgment at Nuremberg' thing. Nor the time. Look at the calendar. Within a week the Siberian winds will sweep down on North Korea. The people will be freezing and hungry and leaderless."

"They'll need food and fuel to get through the winter and only Russia and China are close enough to provide it," Charlie said. "We could reimburse them for part of it later."

"It's 'Let's Make a Deal' time," Carlos said. "Stop nagging Russia over East Ukraine, Crimea, and Syria and China over the China Sea islands and their trade gimmicks, in return for big time instant help for North Korea."

"It would be in China and Russia's best interest to supply North Korea with food, fuel, and other material to get through this first winter," General Callahan said. "Otherwise, the North Koreans would be tempted to take some of it. Their army may still be one-half million strong."

"South Korea needs to help too," Carlos said, "but the last thing you need is for there to be shooting. Maybe if we can get the U.S., China and Russia together on all this we can return to the strategic concept of security of peace through a balance of power arrangement.

< 97 >

Remember the war of the Spanish succession which ended with that peace agreement in seventeen thirteen? Didn't they talk about letting nations have their spheres of influence? That would work better than what we have today where Uncle Sam acts like saving the world is only something he can do alone. And American taxpayers foot the bills."

"General Callahan, do you think South Korea's president would immediately accept North Korean soldiers and their families who know they have relatives in the south that would take them in?" Choe asked.

"Interesting idea, Choe," said Charlie. "Fewer mouths to feed for the north in this terrible time of famine."

"Here's some good news," General Callahan said. "The start of this war was clearly and fully documented as we had recommended. Three ICBMs were launched on a trans-Pacific vector heading our way before our massive counter-stroke was unleashed with lightning speed. It's crystal clear the North Koreans fired first and were clearly targeting the continental U.S. One of those three hit Kansas."

"Democratic leaders are fighting like cats among themselves," Charlie said. "Some want to impeach President Trump for not calling on and waiting for Congress to declare war first. Others see the trap in taking that stance which means accepting sixty million more U.S. citizen casualties. Except for people in the five urban hit zones, Americans seem to be glad the troubles with North Korea are over. As is the rest of the world."

Carlos interjected, "The news this morning is that there were three more ICBMs that hit the continental U.S. in totally uninhabited regions. Most city folks don't know some of our central and western states have big blank places on the map."

Choe spoke up, "Their targeting was terrible. They hit the bottom edge of the New York City metropolitan area, the far east edge of Los Angeles, the far west edge of Kansas City, and the far west edge of Washington DC. Had those nukes been right on target, the casualties would have been quadrupled and the country hamstrung. The three additional uninhabited strike zones were northern Nevada, rural central Alaska and northern North Dakota. Unfortunately, Honolulu was wiped out; that was the only direct hit in their attack. Such a small place on such a small island. Must have been accidental or maybe they were aiming at Pearl Harbor to duplicate the feat of the Japanese."

Choe's eyes misted over, "It was such a beautiful place. My parents

< 98 >

spent their honeymoon in Honolulu and visited it many times."

"Our tracking systems show there were eighteen ICBMs launched. Of these, only eight hit a land target. The others splashed 'target short' into the ocean; lots of them within a thousand miles of North Korea. We think the majority of the long-range ICBM nukes were destroyed in their cradles. Thirty-one more of them. Their battle plan was to first hit the U.S. mainland hard, then launch against our forces and South Korea and Japan with their short and medium range missiles. All that stuff got blown up in their cradles."

Carlos continued, "It was an insane attack plan. You wonder how some of these crazy guys who make history never spent much time reading past history. Kim was in the same place on November twenty-eighth, twenty-twenty that Admiral Yamamoto was in on December seventh, nineteen forty-one. Americans don't know that the Japanese attack on Pearl Harbor was considered by its planners as basically a failure because Yamamoto's goal was to destroy all our aircraft carriers. Yet only one was at Pearl and it was not sunk. He pessimistically commented that he was fearful that they had only awakened a sleeping giant. On November twenty-eighth, twenty-twenty, didn't Kim realize he too was about to 'awaken a sleeping giant'? He was blind to consequences; the shrinks would say he was in denial. Did he doubt all three missiles would reach their targets? Did he think we would 'negotiate' rather than instantly strike back? Did he think we suffered from Obama's latent pacifism? Did he think we had gone soft because we hardly ever execute our most despicable criminals?"

"Carlos," Choe said, "those are good questions for us historians, but for a later time. In the meantime, we should look at our immediate problems here because we've got lots. But it's not nearly as bad as *On the Beach*."

"So far we've been lucky in this beautiful place," General Callahan said. "The winds haven't been blowing our way with their radioactive fallout...yet. If they do, be ready for some panic scenes and ongoing chaos. We are all in for tough times ahead, even in victory. Our people have been advised how to deal with shooters, hurricanes and power outages. In very few places have they prepared people to deal with radioactive fallout. Denial again. Hope someone gets the government and media together quickly to educate people accurately or we'll need martial law even here."

< 99 >

27

CASSANDRA AND THE PEOPLE HELPERS

April 10, 2021
Cassandra Meets the People Helpers

For the last four months the Cassandra Group had been asked to assist with management of martial law and safety/security issues related to radioactive fallout in the five civilian population quarantine zones. There was plenty of legal precedent and historical knowledge about law and safety issues but hardly any useful historical information about radioactive fallout and quarantine.

Legal experts, nuclear physicist and doctors had been accessed and pumped for all potentially useful information. When should people be allowed to leave the nuclear quarantine zone? No one knew for sure. Most believed waiting for six months was necessary. By then, those with a fatal dose would be dead or dying. Lots of semi-healthy people were trying hard to break out of the zone, which was maintained by the National Guard. Some escapees had been successful.

Carlos was particularly interested in the mental health issues in the Washington zone since Sally had started working there the previous week. She worked four days there while living in the National Guard dorm, and commuted home the other three days. On her second day of work she had to use a hammerlock on an unruly male patient and was glad for the self-defense training from Carlos and Choe.

The Cassandra Group had also been consulted occasionally about the joint operation by China, Russia, and the United States for the North Korean Rescue Program which would hopefully continue providing the North Koreans with food aid through September 30, 2021. The United Nations Plebiscite was planned for September 20, 2021 to determine if the North Korean people wanted reconciliation with the south or to remain a separate country.

For historical purposes, the second Korean War began and ended on November 28, 2020. In effect, on November 29, it could

< 100 >

be construed that Delilah and her staff, both here in the Swamp and in Seoul, were out of work. The Searcher goals had been successfully achieved. Mindful of that, Delilah had called Mike Pompeo for further direction and he changed her unit's operational goals. They were given an even tougher assignment: teach North Koreans about self-government, democracy, and all the things the western world thought they knew nothing about. Also, their mandate was to try and stabilize North Korea, to increase food production, and increase economic activity. Of course, they needed a new name to match their new goals. The 'People Helpers' would have to do until a better name came to mind.

Delilah's staff had all tentatively decided to stay at her request although their resumes hardly fit their new goals. Except for Francie's of course.

Francie had immediately suggested her Seoul office send out a letter addressed to the mayors of all town in North Korea or to the chief of their "Hwaback." Hwaback means "harmony of the white-headed"i.e., the Council of Elders. This letter was to explain the United Nations Reconciliation Plebiscite and to ask towns what services they needed most.

In the old days every town had a Council of Elders. Self-government was not unknown to Koreans. Today, no one was sure what political apparatus existed after the extinction of Kim's authoritarianism. Spontaneous self-government? Or chaos? Maybe something "in-between."

Francie, with Delilah's blessing, moved ambitiously into the South Korean political arena and convinced the leaders of a splinter party to introduce a bill to cancel the laws that forbade both Koreas from banning their citizens from contacting each other without government approval. Reunions of South Koreans with their relatives in the north had been done by lottery. But many more had used illegal black market means to more effectively do so. All should now be legal and allowable she argued. When little interest by the South Korean government was shown, she convinced the same party to introduce a bill to ban the sale of candid female pornography, which was big business there, unless the marketeer could prove specific women consented to and were remunerated for the public viewing of their genitalia. This sounded bizarre to lascivious Westerners used to pornography as a capitalist enterprise. In two days, however, Francie got her 'Freedom

< 101 >

of Association' bill, while the government worried over future battles with feminists.

Francie then recruited a band of young people, some who were university students and adept computer hackers and nerds. She oversaw their development of a massive computer-base linking South Korean and North Korean families. At that moment the walls separating the two Koreas came down instantly and dramatically through the power of the Internet.

Meanwhile, Black Hand, now a man without a country, joined with his brother, Red Hand, who had taken over for Francie a small family farm many miles from Seoul in the higher foothills near the North Korean border. They had turned it into a Luther Burbank experimental. They worked with crops like potatoes, yams and squash they believed would do better in the higher, cooler country of North Korea.

In an unexpected development, 67% of North Koreans rejected reconciliation in the UN Plebiscite of September 20, 2021 but favored a government similar to South Korea's. The UN was unhappily forced to set up a three-year timetable for new elections. In the meantime, those North Koreans wishing to go south were encouraged to do so. A people unused to a choice now had too much, or so it was thought. Choice always engenders uncertainty as well as opportunity.

After the Plebiscite, Black Hand said to his brother it was time for the two of them to go north. With Francie's backing Black Hand purchased an abandoned farm in the foothills of Hyesan in North Korea. He and his brother continued their agricultural studies while younger agriculture students from a Seoul university took over Francie's original experimental farm.

Back in the states, Sally was having a tough time in the Washington Fallout Quarantine Zone. It was the Ides of June 2021 and for several weeks the gates of the zone had been thrown open and many National Guard troops were withdrawn. Local state and county law enforcement was taking back their jurisdictions. There was considerable confusion and Sally could tell there was a feeling of jubilation, restlessness and even recklessness among her patients and the general population in the zone. She sensed a danger there and Carlos agreed. Its shape was unclear. Carlos insisted she call him several times a day to check in and report. Sally also called the leadership of the local National Guard only to be surreptitiously laughed at. They

< 102 >

paid more attention when General Callahan called at Carlos' request.

The next morning Carlos called Sally before she was due to leave for work. He said he had an overwhelming feeling that she was in desperate danger and asked her to stay home or at least call someone at work. She phoned her friend Laurel who always went in early. Laurel was tongue-tied and paralyzed with fear and could barely answer yes or no questions but Sally got the picture. The patients had attacked the office, killed the security people, and were systematically raping and looting. Sally reported it to local National Guard headquarters then called Carlos back.

"Sally, I'm coming to get you and bring you home," Carlos said. "The radio here just reported mass disturbance in your quarantine zone. I'll be bringing some heavy hardware courtesy of my crazy friend Mario, and a U.S. Marshal's badge. Keep the handgun I gave you handy and the door propped closed with a chair. If they try and break the door down shoot through it at belt height and reload instantly. I love you...and I'm coming to take you home, my love."

When Carlos got to Sally's door there were two suitors ahead of him, lying dead to the world.

By sunset Sally was safely home. Once there, Carlos gave her a big hug and held her close to him for an hour, until the shaking stopped.

< 103 >

28

CHRISTMAS AT THE RED DRAGON, 2024

Saturday before Christmas, 2024
The Red Dragon Restaurant

By Christmas all four members of the Cassandra Group and all members of the People Helpers had been given informal notice that their services would not be needed by incoming President Perez's very active 'advance troops'.

General Callahan said, "Our democracy survived Trump, it will survive Perez." He suggested they hang on to their jobs until receiving official notice but dust off their resumes and start looking. He also suggested a yearly reunion at the Red Dragon the Saturday before Christmas at seven in the evening. That tradition lasted thirteen years but ended with General Callahan's death. Mary Lou was devastated, as were all his friends.

Carlos and Sally moved to a tiny university-provided apartment in a historic house at Stanford. They spent summers horseback riding and hiking at the Rancheria in New Mexico.

Charlie became an American citizen and he and Delilah raised a boy and a girl. Charlie was a history professor at Harvard and Delilah worked for her daddy's corporate headquarters in Boston earning three times Charlie's salary. That was after her two terms as governor of the state of Massachusetts.

Darlene, who had been mentored by Delilah into a smart, confident young woman fell in love with Choe. Choe married her and brought her to live in Korea. Sometimes south, sometimes north. Choe, following in the big footsteps of his baby sister Francie, went into politics. When Darlene showed an interest in a career in mixed martial arts, Choe encouraged. Within a year Darlene was a sensation in South Korea and the sports world. In his spare time Choe was a Wongwang scholar.

< 104 >

In 2050 Francie became President of North Korea. She asked Carlos to be Ambassador to the United States. He accepted.

Valerie Cummings obtained a PhD in History from the University of Chicago and married a gynecologist.

Carlos and Sally were peak personalities in the 2050 DC social scene. He was the author of *Historical Highlights of the 21st Century*, and she the author of *Psychotherapy for the Nuclear Survivor*. Sally was still a stunner, and so was Teresa's jewelry.

< 105 >

29

At Peace in Pyongyang

November 28, 2070/3:00 p.m.
The Pyongyang Peace Garden

Pyongyang had been totally incinerated exactly fifty years before. It had not yet arisen again like a phoenix from the ashes. Yet stubborn mankind had rebuilt a tiny piece of this place as a starting point for the Pyongyang of the future. Massive amounts of rock, soil, and gravel were compacted on a small knoll on the edge of the old city. The gardens had opened officially today to the whole world but with still a little discrimination. No one younger than seventy was allowed here since the background radiation was still not considered safe for the young who had reproductive and other such assets to protect.

This amazing human accomplishment was the work of the Rejuvenus Corporation, which started out back in the twenties doing rehab work for the Washington DC area Nuclear Quarantine Zone.

In 2042 and for the next fifteen years, they worked in India and Pakistan to heal some of the scars of the Kashmir nuclear confrontation. In 2058 they were hired to make a beachhead restoration in Pyongyang along with the cleanup of various nuke/ICBM sites in North Korea which were closest to the South Korean border. The opening of the Pyongyang Peace Garden in 2070 was the biggest social-political event of that year.

It had the look of a geriatric ward. Attendees consisted of dignitaries, the media and the cops. Old guys and gals were everywhere.

Two tired old men pushing a third dying man in a wheelchair, arrived just as the ceremony finished, as was their plan. To get in one of them showed a gold-embossed invitation from the president of the Rejuvenus Corporation; it was an entrance ticket usually accorded only to heads of state. The holder of this letter had known and worked with the president fifty years before.

< 106 >

The old guys slowly walked around the beautiful, lush little garden and returned to the memorial marker where they left a wreath of flowers and greens with a little card that read:

Good Life to Pyongyang. May Feng Shui favor you once again. With love from Carlos, Choe, Charlie, and Friends.

< 107 >